**"You're the se...**
**Anna, do you...**

Oliver's voice had gone so low it sent shivers down her spine, her toes curling in her shoes. "I want you in my bed tonight. I can't live with you and not have you. It's driving me insane."

Anna's hopes took a nosedive. He couldn't have made it any plainer what he wanted from her if he'd spelled it out in letters ten feet high. "If you can't handle my presence then perhaps I shouldn't stay."

"You can't mean that, Anna."

"Why can't I?"

"Because—because things are good between us."

"Like sex, you mean?" she asked acidly.

She tried to forget that it was all she'd thought about when she'd first met him. There had been an instant chemical flare of attraction, of desire, of goodness knew what, which they'd both mistaken for love.

Which was still there! But it wasn't enough....

Born in the industrial heart of England, **MARGARET MAYO** now lives in a Staffordshire countryside village. She became a writer by accident, after attempting to write a short story when she was almost forty, and now writing is one of the most enjoyable parts of her life. She combines her hobby of photography with her research.

# Margaret Mayo

## THE WIFE SEDUCTION

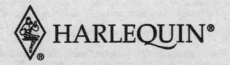

HARLEQUIN®

TORONTO • NEW YORK • LONDON
AMSTERDAM • PARIS • SYDNEY • HAMBURG
STOCKHOLM • ATHENS • TOKYO • MILAN • MADRID
PRAGUE • WARSAW • BUDAPEST • AUCKLAND

ISBN 0-373-18775-0

THE WIFE SEDUCTION

First North American Publication 2002.

Copyright © 2000 by Margaret Mayo.

Visit us at www.eHarlequin.com

**Printed in U.S.A.**

# CHAPTER ONE

'ARE you happy?'

Anna snuggled up against Oliver, feeling the exciting heat of his body, and nodded. This was a holiday romance come true. Two weeks in her sister's cottage with the handsome Oliver Langford and she was head over heels in love. They were now on the ferry on their way home to England and he'd asked her to marry him and she truly was the happiest girl in the world. She wasn't sure Oliver even needed to ask whether she was happy. Wasn't it there in the glow on her face, in the way she looked at him, kept touching him, kept rubbing her body against him? He was incredible. He was magnificently male, and she never wanted to let him go.

Meeting him on the outward trip and then having him turn up on the doorstep a few days later had been totally amazing, like something out of a movie. How he'd found her, she didn't care. It was sufficient that he had. She'd had no hesitation about inviting him in and then asking him to stay for the rest of her holiday.

He was totally, mind-numbingly gorgeous. The proverbial tall, dark handsome stranger, with an incredible magnetism and the most amazing tawny-gold eyes.

That never-to-be-forgotten crossing from Fishguard to Rosslare had been rough, the ferry objecting to the buffeting waves, and when Anna cannoned into

Oliver Langford in the gift shop his arms had come instinctively and protectively around her.

Immediately, without any warning, an electric current had shot through her. She felt an instant and unaccountable response, a scary response. Nothing like that had ever happened to her before.

'I'm sorry,' she'd stammered, finding it hard to even speak. It was as though the air around them had thickened, making it impossible to breathe—as though a cloud had shut out everyone else in the gift shop, insulating her and the stranger in a cocoon of sensuality.

'The pleasure's mine.' There had been a gruffness in his voice as though he too had felt his senses stirred by the sudden impact, as though he too was aware of no one around them.

He couldn't seem to drag his eyes away from her; they were dipping deep into her soul and searching for answers to questions that she knew nothing about. They were looking hungrily at her mouth and back to her eyes again.

'Would you like me to walk you back to your seat?' And still his golden eyes were locked into hers. It was as though he were consuming her, filling Anna with a fever of desire such as she had never felt before.

How could a perfect stranger do that? It didn't make sense. Why should the impact of a man dressed all in black spin her into a sexual frenzy?

There was no answer.

She'd wrenched away from him. 'I can manage,' she'd said with quiet dignity, not realising how much fire there was in her emerald eyes, or what it was doing to the man who had saved her from falling.

She'd gone quietly back to her seat and hadn't seen him again until he turned up at the cottage. Not that she hadn't thought about him. She had, constantly, and the shock of seeing him had almost sent her into a blind panic, it was as though she had conjured him up by simply thinking about him.

But those two weeks had been the most unforgettable of her life. She'd gone to that beautiful corner of southern Ireland for peace and relaxation after a job gone wrong and instead had found passion and excitement beyond measure, which had climaxed in Oliver asking her to marry him.

'What are you thinking?' Oliver stroked Anna's delightful retroussé nose with a gentle finger. Fate was at last being kind to him. Anna was so much the antithesis of other women he had known that he couldn't believe his good fortune.

She turned her face up to his, her green eyes smiling, her silky red hair a perfect foil for her porcelain pale skin with its scattering of freckles which he had kissed—every single one of them—and thoroughly enjoyed doing so.

'I was thinking about how we met,' Anna admitted. 'About the stunning quickness of it all. Two weeks ago I didn't know you, and now I've promised to marry you. Am I out of my mind?'

'If you are then so am I,' he told her with a tender smile. 'Two weeks ago I was off women altogether. You are a very special person, Anna Paige, do you know that? I think you must be a witch in disguise, casting your magic spell over me. And I think we should make our wedding arrangements the moment we get home.'

'You don't think we should wait and make sure?' she asked softly.

'I am sure,' he declared. 'I want to spend the rest of my life with you. I want to make babies with you. I want—everything. Your love, your devotion, your friendship, your commitment. It's what I'm prepared to give you. Am I asking too much?'

He held his breath as he waited for her answer.

To his relief Anna smiled and offered her mouth for his kiss. 'It's what I want as well,' she whispered and he could feel the passion trembling through her.

If they hadn't been in a public place he would have made love to her. Contenting himself with a kiss was a poor second. She was so ravishing, he couldn't keep his hands off her.

It had been blind panic that had made him follow her off the ferry. The thought of never seeing her again had made him feel quite ill, and he had cursed the conference that kept him away from her for three days.

He had told himself he was crazy because he'd never felt such an instant mind-blowing attraction to a woman before, and he'd kept imagining her with another man. He couldn't believe that someone as radiant and beautiful as Anna did not have a boyfriend.

It had been with a great deal of trepidation, therefore, that he had knocked on the cottage door. And a dream come true when he discovered she was alone—and equally as pleased and excited to see him.

'Quite how soon are you proposing we should get married?' she asked huskily.

'At the very first opportunity,' he growled, savouring the sweetness of her mouth, breathing in the very essence of her which drugged his senses every time she was near. In fact, she continually drove him crazy. Even thinking about her when they were apart, for no matter how short a space of time, minutes even, his male hormones rioted. He was in a constant state of excitement. 'I can't take the risk that someone else will come along and snatch you from me.'

'There's no chance of that,' she told him with a sweetly confident smile. 'You've bewitched me too.'

But he intended taking no chances. Their wedding was going to take place as speedily as he could arrange it. Never before had he met a woman who he safely knew he wanted to spend the rest of his life with. Anna was different, he knew that instinctively, and he didn't want to waste precious time.

As soon as they docked he planned to take her home to Cambridge to meet his father, and he was hoping Anna would stay overnight before returning to her rented London flat. He was terrified that out of sight would mean out of mind, only reluctantly accepting that she needed to sort and finalise things before she came to live with him.

These two passionate weeks in Ireland had taught him how precious she was to him, how much a part of him she had become, so that without her even breathing was difficult.

What he wasn't prepared for, but on hindsight knew that he should have been, was his father's reaction.

\*    \*    \*

'Father, I'd like you to meet Anna Paige, the girl I'm going to marry.'

Anna beamed at Edward Langford. He was not quite as tall as his son and much heavier set, but he had the same lion's eyes and a mass of long thick white hair brushed back from his face like a mane.

She held out her hand but to her amazement he didn't take it. Instead his eyes were fierce and condemning, visibly rejecting her.

She had no idea why. And after looking her up and down with a contemptuous curl to his lip, as though she were not fit to even be in the same room, he directed his attention back to his son. 'Are you out of your mind, Oliver?'

She felt Oliver stiffen and her hand sought his. What was going on here?

'No, Father, I'm not,' he answered firmly. 'I love Anna.'

'Love! Bah! How long have you known her?'

'Two weeks.' Oliver's hand tightened over Anna's, reassuring her, silently telling her that his father's bark was worse than his bite and not to be alarmed. 'But time doesn't enter into it. I love Anna, and it doesn't matter what you say, Father, I'm going to marry her—as soon as I can arrange it. I see no reason to wait.'

'You're a fool.' The older man's face was furiously red by this time.

Anna finally spoke. 'If he is then I'm a fool, too. I feel the same as Oliver, I want to marry him without delay. I'm sorry you feel this way, Mr Langford, but I can assure you that—'

She was interrupted by Edward's housekeeper saying that he was needed on the telephone urgently because there was trouble at one of the sites.

'You see to it,' Edward ordered Oliver peremptorily. 'Heaven knows, there have been enough problems while you've been away.'

Oliver looked down at Anna and frowned and she knew he was worried about leaving her. 'It's all right,' she said with a confident smile. He'd already told her that his father had retired from his property development company because of heart problems and handed over the reins to him, so it was only right and proper that Oliver deal with things now.

'Have you any real idea why my son's asked you to marry him?' Edward thundered, the moment Oliver left the room.

The question sent her brows sliding up but she refused to be intimidated. 'Because he loves me, Mr Langford, as I do him. Are you suggesting there is any other reason?'

'I'm not suggesting it, I know it,' he told her grimly. 'He's in love with someone else. Admittedly they had a dispute and Oliver told her it was all over, but he's said that before, more than once, and they've always got back together.'

'Would her name be Melanie, by any chance?' asked Anna sharply.

Edward Langford's bushy brows rose. 'He's told you about her?'

Anna inclined her head. 'Naturally. We've kept nothing from each other. A good marriage has to be based on trust and understanding and we've been perfectly open about our past lives.' She had told Oliver about Tony, the guy she was once engaged to, and he'd told her about Melanie, the girl his father wanted him to marry.

'You've caught him on the rebound.'

'I don't think so,' Anna retorted. 'Oliver said it was definitely all over.' He had added that he was glad to get rid of her. She was the daughter of a close friend of Edward's, and his father's god-daughter to boot. Oliver had found out that she was bragging to her friends about what a good stud he was and that she could get as much money as she liked out of him.

'How do you know that I'm not just after your body as well?' Anna had taunted. And even as she spoke she'd rubbed herself against him, slid down the zip on his trousers and slipped her hand inside. He had groaned and succumbed and it had been a long time before they finished their conversation, a very long time.

'My son's had enough fortune-hunters on his tail for me to be able to spot them a mile off,' insisted Edward Langford, looking at Anna with such dark intent that she shivered.

'You're just a little more clever than most,' he snarled. 'You got in when he was at his most vulnerable. But his money is my money. He's worked his way up in my company, I made sure he did it the hard way, but every penny he earns is indirectly from me, and I will not allow some—hussy—to come along and take it from him.'

Anna eyed the old man coolly, not allowing the light to fade from her eyes for one millisecond. 'When I met Oliver, Mr Langford, I didn't know he came from a wealthy family, or even that he had money himself. I fell in love with Oliver the man. He could have been unemployed, for all I cared. Money doesn't interest me, except as a need to buy clothes for my back and food for my stomach. So long as I have enough for that, I'm quite happy.'

Faded golden eyes looked hostilely into her sparky green ones, her words not impressing him in the slightest. 'I'm expected to believe that, am I? Well, let me tell you, miss, there's not one woman alive who isn't impressed by money.'

He crossed to a desk, whipped out a cheque book and scribbled in it before ripping out the cheque and offering it to her. 'Here, take this, and let that be an end to this impossible situation.'

It was for an indecently large amount, enough to set her up for the rest of her life, but Anna wasn't interested. In fact, she was insulted by his offer. All she wanted was to marry the man she loved.

Her eyes flashed her indignation; her spine stiffened. 'I don't want your money, Mr Langford. I realise that you don't believe in love but I do, and so does Oliver, and all we want is to be together.' Slowly and deliberately she tore the cheque into tiny pieces and let them flutter to the ground. 'This is what you can do with your money.'

The golden eyes leapt with fire, but to give him his due the old man remained coldly distant. 'You're a silly little girl,' he spat. 'You're making the biggest mistake of your life.'

'I don't think so,' she told him calmly. 'But you're entitled to your opinion.'

Wide nostrils flared even wider. 'If I cannot persuade you to change your mind about this impossible marriage then be warned, if you ever do anything to hurt my son, Miss Paige, anything at all, then you'll have me to contend with. Make no mistake about that.'

When Oliver came back into the room she was alone, the torn cheque tucked into the bottom of her bag for disposing of later.

'Where's my father?' he asked with a frown.

Anna shrugged. 'I guess he found something else to do.' She didn't want to spoil things by telling him what his father had done.

'I'm so sorry he didn't give you the welcome you deserve,' he said, pulling her close and looking worriedly into her eyes. 'I truly never expected he'd react like this.'

'It doesn't matter,' she said. 'You're the one I'm marrying; you're the one I love.'

'Let's go home,' he growled. 'There are things I want to do to you.'

Anna's body leapt in response and she wasn't sorry to be walking out of Weston Hall. It was the family home, a daunting square brick house built on a vast estate on the outskirts of Cambridge.

Oliver lived at Weston Lodge in the grounds. Near enough to his father in case Edward needed him, but far enough away to live his own life.

'I like it here,' she said happily as they walked inside. It was still a fairly large house but nothing like the Hall. It had a warm and welcoming atmosphere with spacious rooms and plenty of plump comfy armchairs. 'Is this where we'll be living when we're married?'

'It certainly is, and it's where we'll be spending

tonight. In fact—' his eyes darkened dramatically '—I think I should show you the bedroom straight away.'

Anna had no qualms about that. She pushed the unhappy episode with his father out of her mind and got on with the job of loving Oliver Langford.

## CHAPTER TWO

IT WAS a perfect spring morning, daffodils nodding, birds singing, the sky a deep heavenly blue. The church was massed with flowers—white flowers, every sort imaginable, roses, lilies, carnations—and white satin bows and trailing ribbons; as Anna walked up the aisle on her father's arm she had never felt happier.

Oliver had taken so much trouble to ensure their marriage was perfect in every detail. All she'd had to do was choose her wedding dress and her young niece's bridesmaid's dress. Oliver and her parents had done the rest. How they'd achieved so much in a week she wasn't sure.

There was a vast difference between the welcome her parents had given Oliver to the way Edward had threatened her. She had deliberately pushed his hostility to the back of her mind, telling herself that it was only a matter of time before Oliver's father accepted her, but she couldn't help thinking about it sometimes.

Oliver turned as she reached him and the light of love in his eyes had never burned so bright. 'You look beautiful,' he praised softly, 'like one of Titian's mythical figures. I am the world's luckiest man.'

'I'm lucky, too,' she whispered. 'I love you, Oliver Langford.'

His father didn't attend their wedding but it didn't

16

mar the day for Anna. In fact if Edward had been
there she would have been too aware of his resentment to relax. Instead everything was perfect.

As Oliver had important business commitments
they postponed their honeymoon but Anna didn't
mind. She felt as though they'd honeymooned already. Those magical days and nights in Ireland
would live in her memory for ever, and in the months
that followed she had never been happier.

Oliver was completely happy too. He showed it in
so many ways. He certainly wasn't pining for a lost
love.

Her brother had been unable to attend their wedding
because of business commitments in Europe, but now
he was back and she was delighted when he paid her
a surprise visit.

They looked nothing like brother and sister. Chris
was older by five years, had blond hair rather than
red, and eyes which were a deep navy blue. He was
tall and seriously good looking.

He ran his own advertising company and adored
his younger sister. 'What a pity Oliver isn't here,' she
said. 'I really want you to meet him. Come in, sit
down: we have so much to catch up on.'

Chris looked surprisingly serious all of a sudden.
'I actually knew Oliver wouldn't be home. It's the
reason I came now, while you're alone.'

Anna frowned, some of her happiness evaporating,
a vague unease taking its place. 'Why? Don't you
approve? Have you come to warn me about him? Is
there something you've found out that I don't know?'

He gave a faint, tight-lipped smile, an awkward

smile. 'Of course not, silly. I need to ask you a favour, a big one.'

'Oh?' This was a turn-up for the books. It was usually Anna asking Chris for something. She was the baby of the family and he'd always been good to her.

'There's no easy way to say it.' He bit his lip reflectively and recrossed his ankles several times. 'I need money, Anna.'

'What?' She'd never known Chris short of money.

'My business is in trouble,' he announced unhappily. 'Although—' he added quickly, before she could say anything '—I'm expecting a big order which will set me right back on track. It's just a hiccup, but—' he spread his hands expansively '—without financial help I could go under.'

Anna shook her head, desperately sorry for Chris. 'I don't see how I can help—unless you were thinking that Oliver might?' she asked in a moment of enlightenment. 'In fact, I'm sure he would; he's the most generous man I know. I could ask him.'

'No!' Chris virtually jumped down her throat. 'You must never tell your husband.'

And when Anna looked shocked, he explained ruefully, 'You see, the order I'm hoping to get, which I'm sure I will get, is from your husband's company. And if he knew I was having difficulties then he'd never put the business my way. Unless—' a sudden thought struck him '—he already knows who I am? If so, I'm sunk.'

'He knows I adore you,' she answered with one of her wide sparkling smiles, 'and he knows you're in advertising—but I don't think I've ever mentioned the name of your company.'

His shoulders relaxed and he let out a long-held breath. 'Thank goodness.'

'I could give you a few hundred, I suppose,' she said slowly, thoughtfully. 'What were you thinking of?' But when he told her how much he needed, more if she'd got it, she gave a groan of despair. 'I don't have that kind of money. Have you tried Mum and Dad? They had an endowment policy up recently, I bet—'

'I can't,' he said, running his fingers agitatedly through his hair. 'You know how much Dad was against me going into business for myself, said I hadn't got the head for it. If I told him I was in trouble I'd never hear the last of it.'

Anna sighed. 'There is one possible solution. Oliver puts some money into an account for me each month, I don't know why; I told him I don't need it. There's enough in there. Although actually I'd promised myself I'd never touch it; I don't want him to think I married him for his money.' She didn't want to be tarred with the same brush as Melanie, or to give Oliver's father the ammunition he was looking for.

'Anna, I promise you'll get it back.' Chris leaned forward eagerly, his navy eyes brightening with hope. 'Oliver need never know.' And he'd gone on pleading until in the end she'd reluctantly given in.

And no one would have been any the wiser if Edward Langford hadn't seen her brother leaving the house, hadn't seen him giving her a hug on the doorstep...

A few days went by before Oliver confronted her. He'd given her no clue over dinner as to what was to come, but when she got up to clear the table—something she always did for Mrs Green—he said, 'Sit down again.' And his tone brooked no refusal.

Anna stared at him in amazement because he never, ever, spoke to her like this. 'What's wrong?' His face was frighteningly grim all of a sudden.

'I hear you had a visitor a few days ago, a male visitor.' Well-shaped brows rose questioningly. 'I've been waiting for you to tell me about him, but since it's clear that you're not going to, then I'm afraid I shall have to insist on knowing who it was.' His golden eyes were accusing and hard and in that moment he looked very much like his father.

Anna gave an inward groan. This was what came of promising to keep secrets. 'Who told you?'

'My father, as a matter of fact,' he answered icily. 'Not that it really matters who told me. The point is, you didn't.'

She might have known Edward would find out. He probably permanently spied on her, or had someone do it for him. 'And what did your father have to say?' she asked defensively. 'That I'm having an affair?' It was exactly what Edward Langford would like her to do. Anything to end their marriage.

'I'm asking you to explain who he was. It stands to reason that if it was something innocent you'd have told me.'

'As a matter of fact it was innocent,' she claimed, her green eyes sparking angry fire. 'It was my brother.' And that was as much as he needed to know.

There was a sceptical lift now to those dark brows.

'Your brother? And you didn't tell me?' He made her sound stupid.

'I guess it slipped my mind,' she replied with a faint shrug, wondering why she found him amazingly sexy when he was angry.

Oliver shook his head in disbelief. 'Your brother comes home after months abroad and it slips your mind? Do you take me for an idiot? It would be the first thing you'd tell me.' He stood up and hauled Anna to her feet, his hands gripping her shoulders so hard that they hurt. 'I want the truth. Who was it? Was it that swine of a man you were once engaged to? Is he hanging around again?'

'Tony?' Anna was dismayed that Oliver would even think this way. 'I've not seen him since we split up and that's the truth. I should have said something, I know, but you weren't here when I thought about it, and when you were—well, we had other things to occupy our minds.' She moved her body suggestively against his. 'Much more interesting things. I love you, Oliver, far too much to be unfaithful. I'll never, ever, do that to you, I promise.'

He groaned and his mouth came down on hers. 'I told my father he was wrong, I said you weren't like that, but—oh, Anna—' and words weren't needed to express his sorrow for doubting her.

'You'd better invite your brother over here one evening,' he muttered between kisses.

And Anna agreed, while knowing she would keep putting it off until after Chris got the order.

Their lovemaking that night was quick and intense. The argument had heightened their senses and the instant Oliver touched her she exploded, feeding herself from his mouth in a frenzy of sexual hunger.

His hands were all over her, fierce and encouraging, and Anna's nails clawed Oliver's back as he found the moist, throbbing heart of her. She arched her body in glorious wild abandonment. 'Take me now, Oliver. Now!'

It was the best time ever. She jerked and bucked beneath him and thought the waves of pleasure would never stop. Oliver too groaned and shuddered, and they went to sleep in each other's arms, completely satisfied.

A week or so later an excited Chris phoned her. 'I've got the business, Anna. Can you meet me? I want to take you out for a celebratory lunch.'

That lunch proved her undoing.

The very same evening Oliver came home from work with his face grim, his eyes so hard and condemning that Anna knew exactly what he was going to say. And he didn't fail her. 'I want to know who you had lunch with today.'

Her shoulders stiffened. 'How do you know I had lunch with anyone?' And because attack was always the best form of defence, she added angrily, 'Have you been spying on me? Don't you trust me any more? If this is what I'm going to get from you every time I go out, then—'

He sliced through her words. 'Who was he?'

A feeling of unease seeped into Anna's bones. 'It was Chris again, as a matter of fact.'

'The mystery brother who you seem determined I shouldn't meet?' His voice was loaded with sarcasm, his golden eyes razor-sharp. 'I don't believe you, Anna.'

Her hackles began to rise. 'I'm sorry, but it's the truth.'

'So when were you planning to tell me? Or was this to be another of your little secrets?' he asked sarcastically. 'I suddenly don't understand you, Anna. In fact, I feel I don't know you at all.'

Anna sighed deeply and unhappily. Even though her brother had asked her to keep quiet a while longer, she knew that it wouldn't be wise, that it was time to tell Oliver the truth. It couldn't hurt, surely, not now that Chris had got the order?

She hadn't liked keeping it a secret from her husband, and she liked even less the way he was accusing her. But before she could even open her mouth, Oliver sprang another surprise accusation.

'Not only are you dating another man but you're giving him money.' His golden eyes blazed with fury. 'Money that I, out of the generosity of my heart, have given you.'

A flash of righteous anger ripped through Anna. 'You've checked up on me? How dare you? You had no right.' If she was a man she'd have punched him. It was an invasion of privacy, that's what it was— even though he'd given her the money in the first place.

'Unless what you're saying is that the money isn't really mine,' she flared. 'Is that it? It's just a token thing to make you look good and feel good, but you never intended that I should spend any of it. And now that it's gone you're wishing you'd never given it to me in the first place.'

'My actions are not in question,' he retorted coolly. 'What is, is why have you given away thirty thousand pounds. It's what I'm assuming you've done with it. Or have you spent it on some flash piece of jewellery that you've not yet shown me? I don't think so. There's a man involved and I want to know who he is and what he means to you. And don't continue to give me that brother rubbish, because it won't wash.'

Before Anna could say anything in her own defence, he added, 'It's that rat you were once engaged to, isn't it? An ambitious but penniless young man, you said, who didn't want to be tied down into marriage before he'd made his millions. Is this his way of doing it, sponging off other people?'

'You're crazy, Oliver Langford.' There were two spots of high colour in Anna's cheeks, her eyes were brilliant with anger. 'This has nothing to do with Tony. Actually, it has nothing to do with you, either.' Brave words. 'That money was mine to do with as I liked—or so I thought. If you have a problem with that, if you can't trust me enough to accept that I had a very good reason for doing what I did, and that one day I would have told you, then you're not half the man I thought you were.'

'Oh, so you would have told me?'

'Eventually.'

'In my book, husbands and wives don't keep secrets from each other.'

She tossed her head, red hair flying magnificently. 'If you hadn't been nosy enough to check up on me, you wouldn't have known. And if you saw me at lunchtime, why the hell didn't you come and speak to me? Or do you get some sort of savage enjoyment out of spying on me?'

Anna couldn't believe they were having this conversation, that their idyllic marriage was in danger because of a promise she'd made to her brother.

'It wasn't me who saw you, it was my father.'

'Ah!' She needed to hear no more. 'And I suppose he couldn't wait to tell you? To blacken my name? I suppose he also made a point of saying that he saw my companion with his arms around me as we parted? It must have looked a very cosy scene to him.'

She shook her head in wild and furious resentment. Edward Langford would have her hung, drawn and quartered without an ounce of compassion, or any thought that he could have been wrong. She'd played right into his hands.

This was exactly what he'd been hoping for.

Their argument raged long and loud until eventually Oliver walked out. Where he went she didn't know, but he didn't come home that night. And the bed felt cold and empty without him.

At lunch time the next day he turned up and began ramming clothes and toiletries indiscriminately into a holdall. 'You'll see me again when you're prepared to tell me the truth,' he said icily, almost viciously, 'and not a minute before.'

The days that followed were the blackest of Anna's life. She was aware that her husband had moved in with his father because she'd seen his car whizzing past, and she kept expecting Oliver to walk through the door and say he'd made a mistake, that he loved her and couldn't live without her, but he didn't. And she had too much pride to go after him.

Besides, she was hardly likely to be made welcome there. Edward would continue to feed his son's distrust and anger—until in the end he'd have no love left for her at all.

When Edward himself came to visit she wasn't surprised, in fact, she'd been expecting it. But what he had to say most certainly did shock her.

'I want you out of this house,' he said bluntly.

'I think that's up to your son.' Anna surprised herself by managing to keep her voice cool and calm, her chin high. 'As far as I'm concerned, we're still married and I have every right to live here. I'm afraid it has nothing to do with you.'

'Really?' Shaggy brows rose to meet the mane of white hair. 'Perhaps Oliver omitted to mention that this house actually belongs to me. And in that event I have every right to evict you. I'm giving you seven days to find somewhere else to live.'

Anna felt as though he'd stabbed her between the shoulder blades. Oliver had never breathed a word about his father owning Weston Lodge. For pity's sake, why had he never bought a place of his own? It wasn't as though he couldn't afford it. It didn't make sense.

But it was herself she had to think about now. She was jobless and virtually penniless and in a week's time she would be homeless. Edward must have laughed his head off when Oliver walked out on her.

Anna supposed she could move in with her own parents, but they'd been so pleased she'd found such a wonderful man after her disastrous engagement to

Tony that she couldn't bear to tell them it was all over so quickly.

She could also go to see Oliver and plead with him, go to see him at the office in order to avoid Edward, but pride stood in her way. Oliver had made his position very clear and if he wanted her back then he was the one who had to do the running.

So she moved to her sister's holiday cottage—the very place where she'd first met Oliver. Damn him! She'd expected at the very least a courtesy call before she left Weston Lodge—but no. Nothing. Not a visit, not a phone call, not even a hastily written note on a scrap of paper saying good riddance.

Actually this cottage was the worst place she could have come to. It was filled with too many memories. It was here that they'd introduced themselves properly, here where they'd first made love, here where they'd fallen in love. Just the thought of Oliver making love to her sent her into a tizzy.

But she'd had little choice of where to live at such short notice. She'd taken her sister into her confidence and Dawn had offered her the cottage for as long as she needed it.

'Although if I know Oliver,' Dawn had said, 'he'll be after you in no time at all, begging you to go back to him. That guy's deeply in love with you. You can't tell me that some stupid misunderstanding will change it. Once Chris's business is on the up, and you're free to tell Oliver the truth, then—'

'I don't think so.' Anna shook her head with fierce determination. 'I'm certainly not going to run after him with explanations.'

'But—' began Dawn.

'But nothing,' interrupted Anna. 'I've made up my mind. And I don't want you to tell Chris what's happened either, or he'll feel truly awful. Tell him, if he asks, that Oliver has business in Ireland and we're using your cottage. Tell Mum and Dad that as well.'

In the weeks that followed she tried to convince herself that she was well rid of Oliver, but the truth was she missed him more than she had imagined possible. She missed their nights of passion—sleeping alone was crucifying her, she missed his companionship, their long, interesting, sometimes heated conversations. In those six short months he had become so much a part of her life that she found it difficult living without him, it was as though half of her was missing.

Time would heal she supposed—but...

It was obvious his love for her had died—if he'd ever truly been in love with her. Maybe his father was right and he had turned to her on the rebound.

Perhaps it had been lust that drove him, some sort of physical cleansing to rid his mind of the woman who had hurt him. The physical side of their marriage had certainly been a very high priority—not that she'd complained, she'd been as eager as he to satisfy their pagan needs.

And then came the phone call. Only Dawn ever rang so it was a distinct shock to hear Oliver's deeply attractive voice. A surge of something approaching excitement catapulted through her but she stamped on it because it would be fatal thinking along those lines.

Physical reactions were ruinous and negative and must never be allowed purchase. If it was his intention to try and patch things up, he was in for a big disappointment. Oliver Langford had definitely burned his bridges the day he walked out on her.

'Anna, sad news, I'm afraid.' There was no pre-amble.

'Oh?' This wasn't what she'd expected.

'My father died yesterday of a massive heart attack.'

For a few seconds Anna was too stunned to say anything. Edward Langford, dead! The ebullient old man who'd done his best to stop her marriage, gone! She was saddened to hear it even though she hadn't really liked him. The truth was, she'd never been allowed to get to know him.

'I'm sorry to hear that,' she said finally, softly. 'It's hard to take in. He seemed such a vital man, as though he had years of life left in him.'

'My father was his own worst enemy,' Oliver growled. 'He constantly disobeyed doctor's orders. I was wondering if... I—I'd like you to come to the funeral.'

'Of course.' She said it instinctively, then wondered if it would be wise. Edward had turned Oliver against her. Meeting again could invoke friction—and she would hate there to be any of that on the day of his father's funeral. It was likely he was inviting her to keep up a front for the sake of family and friends. He had numerous cousins and aunts and uncles whom she'd never met, who would all be coming to the funeral. And of course there was Melanie!

Anna couldn't help wondering whether Melanie had wormed her way back into Oliver's affections.

# CHAPTER THREE

OLIVER'S palms were moist and there was an unnatural thudding in the region of his heart. Ridiculous when Anna no longer meant anything to him, when he had washed his hands of her and his next planned step was to instruct his solicitor in divorce. How could simply hearing her voice trigger such a juvenile reaction?

He shook his head and forced himself to continue with the very disturbing job of arranging his father's funeral. Edward Langford had died as he had lived. Railing at change, surmising he knew better than everyone else. He'd been arguing with Oliver over the way he was applying new management techniques when he'd keeled over. By the time the ambulance arrived he was dead.

Oliver couldn't bear to remain at the Hall with his father gone and he moved back into the house he had shared with Anna, which wasn't much better because there were memories here of a different kind.

For six months he'd been a completely happy man. He'd found the girl of his dreams, he'd totally adored her and then, like a bullet shattering a crystal vase, his heart had been smashed into a million tiny miserable pieces.

If anyone had warned him that Anna would turn out the same as Melanie, the same as other girls he'd dated, he would have told them they were off their

30

head. Anna was perfection personified; she could do no wrong. Or was that where his problem had lain? He'd stood her on a pedestal, been unprepared for her to have human failings the same as everyone else.

He'd been surprised by her ready acceptance to come to the funeral, and hoped she wasn't trusting he'd had a change of heart. So why, he wondered, had he asked her, if it wasn't to use the opportunity to try and patch things up?

His father had never approved of Anna, the same as he'd never approved of anything Oliver did. All his life it had been like that.

And it would have been perfectly reasonable for him not to ask Anna to come to the funeral. In fact, it would be hard for her to try and pretend sadness for a man who'd never attempted to welcome her into the family.

Technically, though, she was still his wife and he wanted her by his side. None of his family knew that they'd split up, and a funeral was hardly the place to tell them. He steadfastly refused to accept that there was any other reason.

Anna left her car behind and flew to London where Oliver sent a car to pick her up. She'd half-expected that he'd come himself, had felt a flurry of anxiety at the thought, but instead one of his company drivers met her.

Her heart zinged into overdrive as they neared Cambridge but she deliberately hardened it, refusing to accept that she had any feelings left for this man who had so callously walked out on her.

The driver dropped her off at the Lodge, for which

she was grateful. She'd half expected, half dreaded, that Oliver would want her at his father's house with him. And that was something she felt she couldn't face.

If she hadn't been welcome there in his father's lifetime, he wouldn't have wanted her there after his death, that was for sure. But also she needed some breathing space before she confronted Oliver. Time to accustom herself to being back here where she had once been so happy.

His housekeeper was there to greet her. 'It's sad news about Mr Edward,' she said as she busied herself making tea and buttering scones.

'It certainly is,' Anna agreed. 'Is Oliver up at the house? I suppose I ought to—'

'Out on business somewhere,' interrupted Mrs Green. 'There's such a lot to organise.' When the tea was made, the scones pushed towards Anna with a pot of homemade strawberry jam, Mrs Green sat down at the kitchen table and leaned towards her.

'Tell me to mind my own business if you like, but I don't understand why you two split up. I thought you were the perfect couple. Oliver's been like a bear with a sore head. He misses you terribly.'

He had a strange way of showing it, thought Anna. If his father hadn't died, she wouldn't be here now. The next step would have been divorce. She had no doubt in her mind about that.

'He was the one who did the walking, Mrs Green,' she pointed out, not quite meeting the other woman's eyes. 'There's no chance of us getting back together. If that's what you were hoping I'm sorry.'

The woman looked disappointed. 'And I'm sorry it came to this. I'm very fond of you, Anna.'

No more was said and after Anna had nibbled half a scone and drank a cup of tea she got up and began to wander around the house. Nothing had changed. Pictures that she'd chosen were still on the walls, little ornaments, things they'd selected together—everything was exactly as she'd left it.

Upstairs she trailed through the bedrooms, dumping her overnight bag in one of the guest rooms, coming to a sudden halt in the doorway of what had used to be their room.

Anna felt a mixture of trepidation and resignation as she slowly pushed open the door. It turned swiftly to shock. Oliver was back! His leather slippers were tucked beneath the dressing-table stool, a tie hung on the back of a chair, but more potent was the lingering musky smell of his cologne.

When had he returned? After his father's death, or immediately after she had left? What sort of thoughts went through his head as he lay here each night? Was he remembering her and the amazing lovemaking they'd shared—or the way things had used to be before she moved in? Was this what he preferred—the life of a bachelor?

Even as her mind tried to make sense of what she'd just discovered, Anna heard a movement behind her, and whirling round she came face to face with Oliver.

It was a heart-stopping moment. He was as gorgeous as she remembered, his black hair short as though he'd just had it cut, his face a touch gaunt perhaps, his eyes shadowed, but that was perfectly natural under the circumstances. She could imagine how she'd feel if she lost either of her parents.

'Mrs G said I'd find you here. Thank you for coming, Anna; it means a lot to me.'

'It was the least I could do.'

There was an awkward silence and to break it Anna impulsively hugged him. 'I'm sorry about your father.' It was the sort of hug she would give Chris.

But it was a mistake. She had thought she could make it impersonal. Grave error. There was nothing impersonal about her feelings for Oliver. Her mouth ran dry and a mountain of pulses jerked into overtime.

Even Oliver looked stunned, though she couldn't accept that he'd felt anything. More than likely he was wondering what had made her do it, praying she wasn't intent on trying to revive their marriage.

He needn't worry. Whatever feelings ran rampant inside her, she intended to keep them hidden.

'I didn't realise you were living back here,' she said in an effort to defuse the sudden tension.

He offered no explanation, simply saying, 'If you want this room I can easily move—'

'No.' Anna stopped him before he could go any further. 'I've already claimed one of the others. I was just passing the time. I'm sorry if I've intruded.'

She could easily imagine what it would be like sleeping in the bed they had once shared. It was bad enough at the cottage, but here, where they'd spent so many long, deliriously happy months, it would be unbearable. How could he do it?

'So long as you're comfortable.'

Such forced politeness. Best put an end to it. 'I think I might go and unpack and take a shower.'

But he seemed not to want to let her go. 'Carl met you all right?'

'Yes, the plane was on time.'

'I would have come myself but—'

'You had other obligations,' she cut in. 'I understand. This is a sad time for you, Oliver. If there's anything you want me to do, any help I can give, you only have to say.'

'Thank you,' he said and, with an expectant lift of one eyebrow, added, 'Will you have dinner with me this evening?'

This wasn't what Anna had meant and her eyes widened in dismay.

'I'm sorry,' he said at once. 'It's just that I could do with some company right now. But it's all right, I understand how you must feel. I'll cancel the booking and—'

'No, I'll come,' she insisted, feeling sorry for him then.

But later, when she joined Oliver downstairs, when her insides sizzled at the mere sight of him, she began to wish that she'd refused. It was going to be hard hiding the attraction she still held for him.

She guessed that part of it would never go away. She could hate him for what he'd done, the way he'd accused and distrusted her, the way he'd simply abandoned her, but the physical magnetism—that lethal attraction she had felt on the ferry—would always remain.

He was wearing a white shirt and close-fitting dark trousers; his matching jacket lay casually over the arm of a chair. His tie was black and she was reminded how fiercely he must be missing his father.

She herself had chosen to wear a black dress—not purposely in respect for Edward but because it was the only outfit she had brought with her which was suitable for dining out. It had long sleeves and a scoop neck, was fitted to the hips and then flared gently to mid-calf.

Oliver's eyes roved lazily over her, lingering on her mouth, the same sort of appraisal he'd made when they first met and it sent the same sort of dizzy feelings through her, but he made no comment, simply enquiring, 'A drink before we leave, perhaps?'

Anna shook her head. 'No, thank you.' The sooner they went, the sooner they'd be home.

It was a restaurant he'd taken her to before, quietly elegant with tables set far enough apart for conversations not to be overheard. There was no lounge, the bar was in a corner of the dining room, and they were shown straight to their table.

'How did you know where to find me?' she asked after they'd ordered drinks and made their choices from the extensive menu.

'I rang Dawn.' His lips twisted wryly. 'I know you asked her to tell no one but I gave her little choice. Don't be too hard on her.'

Anna actually already knew what he'd done. She'd phoned Dawn last night after Oliver's news about his father, and discovered that Oliver had contacted her sister not long after she'd left for Ireland. The fact that he'd known for all these weeks where she was but done nothing about it spoke volumes.

After the funeral tomorrow he would politely thank her for coming, wish her a safe flight back to Ireland and that would be the end of her marriage.

She had also asked Dawn whether Chris knew that she and Oliver had split up. But her sister had kept her promise in this instance. Anna was aware, though, that the time had come to contact him, her parents too. They had a right to know what was going on.

She'd rung them a couple of times from Ireland but they'd been under the impression that Oliver was with her, and she'd never told them otherwise.

During the meal Oliver steered the conversation away from all things personal, talking mainly about his job, which suited Anna down to the ground. But as he talked she gained the impression that he wasn't happy in his work any more. It wasn't anything he said, just his general attitude. There wasn't the fire and enthusiasm that he'd always had.

Maybe it was because of present circumstances, but somehow she didn't think so. Something had gone wrong that he wasn't telling her about. Which made her sad because he'd always told her everything. She'd congratulated him when things were going well, commiserated if he'd had problems, calmed him when he was angry over something. And now she was no longer a part of that life.

They were halfway through their main course when an attractive blonde wearing a skirt only just long enough to be decent, stopped at their table. 'Oliver, what a surprise.' And, in a very loud aside, 'What's she doing here?'

'Melanie,' he said, politely standing up but not answering her question. 'I thought you were in Egypt.'

'I came back this morning. I couldn't believe it when Daddy told me about Uncle Edward.' There were tears in her eyes as she spoke. 'I tried to phone you. You poor darling, you must be devastated.' She wrapped her arms around him. 'You shouldn't have to bear this alone. If only I'd been here, I—'

'He isn't alone.' Anna heard herself say the words, though they either didn't hear or ignored her. She'd met Melanie a few times and on no occasion had the girl enamoured herself to her. In fact, she had treated Anna with icy disdain.

Anna had always assumed that Oliver continued to put up with her for his father's sake—but when he held her now, when he stroked her hair, almost as though he were comforting Melanie instead of the other way round, Anna felt he was taking things too far. This girl had treated him scandalously, for pity's sake. Why was he behaving like this?

Fury zipped through her veins. Would either of them notice if she got up and walked out? Melanie shouldn't be allowed to do this to Oliver, not after all she'd put him through. Goodness, he'd not even welcomed her, his own wife, with this much fuss.

She stood up, picked up her bag and was halfway across the dining room when Oliver caught her up. 'Where are you going?' he asked quietly.

'To the Ladies.' Because I suddenly feel sick, she added silently.

'You're not walking out because of Melanie? I know she can be a bit full on at times, but for my father's sake I can't ignore her at a time like this.'

'You're a free man,' she tossed airily. 'You can do whatever you like, be with whomever you like. It really doesn't matter to me any more. If you'd prefer Melanie at your side, now she's home from her holiday, then—'

'No!' He said the word sharply and loudly. 'I want you. You are my wife.'

'You walked out on me, Oliver.'

He closed his eyes for a second as if to say, I know and I shouldn't have done. But when he looked at her again his expression was blank, his feelings well hidden. 'Whatever I did, I want you with me now.'

For appearances' sake? she felt like asking, but she didn't. It was the wrong time to goad him. 'I'll be back in a minute,' she said coolly, and carried on to the cloakroom.

But she didn't hasten, taking time to dab powder on her nose and reapply her lipstick. She was running a comb through her hair when the door opened and Melanie waltzed in.

Anna saw her through the mirror, saw the calculating gleam in the blue eyes, and knew immediately that there was trouble brewing. Melanie wasn't here to touch up her make-up, she was spoiling for a fight. Anna turned to face her.

Melanie spoke first. 'I think you have a cheek coming back for Uncle Edward's funeral when Oliver chucked you out.'

'Since Oliver doesn't mind, I hardly think you have any say in the matter,' Anna said with quiet dignity, wondering exactly how much he had told this girl about their break-up. She had no intention, though, of getting into a slanging match. Melanie wasn't worth it.

'Oliver doesn't love you any more.'

It was a childish statement and Anna's finely shaped brows slid up. 'He's told you that, has he?' It was the truth, yes, he had stopped loving her—but she didn't need it ramming down her throat.

'Not in so many words,' Melanie admitted with a careless shrug, taking a brush from her bag and dragging it needlessly through her long thick hair. 'But we've spent a lot of time together since you split up. He needed someone to soothe his ravaged breast,' she added dramatically. 'You could say we're back on to our old footing. He's a fantastic lover, isn't he? The best. I've made sure he's not missing out.'

Surely this couldn't be true? Anna felt her heart take a dive. Oliver wouldn't jump from her bed to Melanie's when he'd declared so strongly that he no longer felt anything for this other girl, would he? Not when Melanie had ruined their relationship with her outrageous bragging.

On the other hand, he was a healthy male with a good appetite for sex; she couldn't expect him to remain celibate for long.

It hurt, though, accepting that he might have turned to Melanie in her absence and it was difficult to remain calm. Somehow she managed it. 'Good for you,' she said with a cool little smile. 'Now, if you'll excuse me, Melanie, I'll get back to Oliver before he thinks we've both deserted him.'

It took even more of an effort to walk to their table and pretend there was nothing wrong. She saw Oliver watching her, frowning, wondering. And she was determined she would give him no cause to ask questions.

'Sorry I took so long,' she said, pasting a brilliant smile on her face.

'What did Melanie have to say?'

'Melanie?' she asked innocently. 'Not a lot. She's very distressed about your father, of course. Is she here on her own? Is she joining us?' She tried to make it sound as though she didn't mind, that she would welcome the other girl.

'I believe she's with a friend,' Oliver told her, his attention distracted as Melanie emerged from the cloakroom. They both watched as the blonde made her way to a table the other side of the room and sat down opposite her male companion with an apologetic smile.

He was a dark-haired, I'm-good-looking-and-I-know-it individual who Anna wouldn't trust as far as she could throw him. A typical rake out for a good time.

How could Oliver bear to touch a woman who went out with men like that? wondered Anna.

'Do you know him?' she asked.

'Who?'

'Melanie's friend. You seemed to be watching them very closely.'

Oliver shrugged. 'Just curious, that's all. I can't say I've ever met the guy—but then, Melanie has lots of friends.'

'She's a very attractive girl.' In an artificial sort of way.

'Mmm, I suppose so.'

'Do you still fancy her?'

'What is this, a third degree?' he asked sharply. 'I've invited *you* out tonight. I don't want to talk about Melanie.'

'But you are very close?' She noticed he hadn't answered her question.

He shrugged. 'She's almost one of the family. I'm glad she's back in time for my father's funeral. She'd have been terribly upset if she hadn't found out until too late.'

'Didn't anyone think to phone her—leave a message at her hotel?'

'No one knew exactly where she was. In Egypt, yes—but precisely where, no. Not even her own father. She has a habit of taking herself off on a whim and telling no one.'

'I see. Did she perhaps holiday with that guy she's with now?'

'I don't know.' Oliver began to sound distinctly irritated. 'And I don't really care. It's no business of mine.'

Oh, but it was, thought Anna. He was getting too worked up to be completely disinterested.

'I want to talk about you,' he said, fixing his eyes steadfastly on hers. 'I want to know why you left so suddenly. I couldn't believe it when my father told me that you'd gone. It didn't make sense. Why didn't you come and see me first?'

So Edward had said nothing about ordering her out, and she could hardly lay the blame now with his father not yet buried. Anna lifted her shoulders in a dismissive gesture. 'What was there to discuss?'

'There was absolutely no need for you to leave,' he declared firmly. 'And why Ireland? I know I was angry with you—damned angry, as a matter of fact— but you didn't have to shoot off like that.'

'I thought it best,' she said quietly.

'And you're happy there?'

Anna shrugged. 'It's temporary.'

'And the boyfriend?'

'What boyfriend?' she asked coldly.

'The one you gave the money to. Is he with you?'

Anna closed her eyes. This was most definitely the wrong time and the wrong place for this kind of conversation. 'You're wrong about Tony but I have no wish to discuss it. I think actually I'd like to go home.' How easily the word slipped out. 'I mean back to your house,' she corrected quickly. 'I'm tired.'

'Very well.' He beckoned the waiter for their bill and surprisingly he never once looked in Melanie's direction as they left the restaurant. But Anna did, and the look of venom in Melanie's eyes was enough to send icy shivers down her spine. The message was clear, this was not going to be the last she saw of her.

# CHAPTER FOUR

ANNA had insisted on going straight to bed when they got back to Weston Lodge despite it being only a little after nine. The fact that Oliver still refused to give her the benefit of the doubt, that he still thought she'd given the money away for personal gain, hurt too much for her to put herself in line for any more accusations. She wanted to spend as little time with him as possible.

She heard him come upstairs a little before midnight, heard him pause at her door, and she waited, wondering if he'd turn the knob and walk in. Her hammered heartbeats echoed in her ears as seconds became a minute and a minute became two.

But finally, much to her relief, he moved on. She heard the faint squeak of the bedroom door—it had always done that and they'd always promised to get it oiled—and the gentle click as it closed. Only then did she realise that she'd been holding her breath.

What had he been thinking as he stood outside? She would have liked to believe that he'd been tempted to come in and make love to her with that driving animal passion which had always set her body on fire. But she knew differently. That part of her life was most definitely over.

Would she ever, though, really know what was going on inside Oliver's head? Was he glad or sorry that their marriage had ended? Was it his intention to file for divorce as soon as the funeral was over? Or did he strongly regret them breaking up but was far too proud to go back on his word?

Dawn was breaking when she finally fell asleep, and when Anna didn't go down for breakfast Mrs Green brought a tray to her room. 'Oliver's orders,' she said firmly as Anna sleepily pushed herself up. 'You have to eat. He said you hardly touched your meal last night. A waste of money, that was; I could easily have cooked you something nice and light.'

'You're very kind, Mrs Green,' said Anna as she lifted the silver cover and saw scrambled eggs, bacon and mushrooms, as well as crisp toast and butter and a pot of marmalade. 'But I'll never get through all this.'

'You've lost weight,' the housekeeper said warningly. 'I bet you haven't been eating properly. Now tuck in like a good girl. I'll put your tea here on the side. Would you like me to pour it?'

'I can manage, thank you.'

No sooner had Mrs Green gone than Oliver walked in. His hair was still damp from the shower, and he was dressed in black trousers and a white silk shirt. He looked sombre and pale and her heart went out to him. 'Did Mrs G pass on my orders?' he asked gruffly.

'It depends what they were,' she replied, taking a fork to the scrambled egg.

'You didn't eat enough last night to feed a sparrow,' he muttered uncompromisingly. 'You haven't been down for breakfast and the funeral's in a little over an hour. What game are you playing?'

Anna felt a pang of horror. 'I hadn't realised how

late it was. I haven't time for breakfast now.' The fork went flying. 'I'll—'

But Oliver was adamant. 'Eat!' he thundered, 'I don't want you fainting on me at the funeral.'

'Only if you leave,' she agreed. 'I can't possibly eat with you standing over me.' Not when it tortured her heart to even look at him.

Family, friends, business colleagues, all were gathered in a hushed group at the cemetery when a lone figure made its way towards them, a tall, elegant, slender woman in her early fifties wearing a smart black suit and a black hat with a wide brim shadowing her face.

Anna had no idea who the latecomer was but she saw Oliver's relatives, especially the older ones, begin to nudge each other and whisper—and not one of them smiled or greeted her.

Oliver was the last to see her, and when he did Anna saw the narrowing of his eyes, the indrawn breath of disbelief, the sudden tightening of his mouth. And when she looked down at his hands they were curled into fists. But it wasn't until they got back to Weston Hall that she found out who the stranger was.

Mrs Green, together with Edward's housekeeper, Mrs Hughes, had prepared a hot buffet and Anna and Oliver stood to one side while everyone helped themselves. Suddenly the woman who had caused such a stir at the cemetery appeared in front of them. Until that moment Anna hadn't even realised that she'd returned to the Hall with the rest of the mourners.

'Oliver,' she cooed, her scarlet lips drawn into the

semblance of a smile. 'What a handsome young man you are. You don't know who I am, of course, but—'

'I know exactly who you are,' he declared in a hard, tight voice. 'What I want to know is what you're doing here?'

The woman laid scarlet-tipped fingers soothingly on his arm. 'What's Edward been saying to you about me? I've come to pay my last respects to my departed husband. There's no crime in that, is there?'

Anna felt her mouth drop open. She'd been given the impression that Oliver's mother was dead. How could this be her?

And yet, looking at her, Anna could see a strong resemblance, especially the fine straight nose and the pronounced shape of their ear lobes. There was no mistaking they were mother and son. In fact, Oliver looked more like his mother than he did his father.

'Except that you're no longer Edward's wife,' he reminded her quietly.

The woman smiled, her vivid lips almost evil. 'Didn't your father tell you, sweetheart, we never got divorced? I know it was more than thirty years ago but we somehow never got round to it. I never married again and neither did Edward so we just—' she gave a shrug of her slim shoulders '—let things drift. You know how it is.'

'No, I'm afraid I don't know how it is,' Oliver retorted, his face visibly paling at this piece of information. 'And I think it would be much better for all concerned if you left—right now.'

But still the woman smiled. 'I can't do that, Oliver. I want to hear what's in the will. Unless you already know the contents?'

Oliver was forced to admit that he didn't. 'My father's solicitor will be coming along later this afternoon to read it.'

'I rather thought that was the way things would be done,' she said. 'Edward had charming old-fashioned views on many things. Why don't you introduce me to—' her pencilled brows rose '—your wife, I believe?'

Reluctantly and gravely Oliver did so. Anna shook the woman's ice-cold hand but as soon as she left to mingle with the others, Anna couldn't help asking, 'Oliver, I thought your mother died when you were little?'

'To all intents and purposes,' he admitted grimly. 'It's what my father wished to believe. Rosemary walked out on him when a business gamble failed; she said he was no good to her without money.'

The money problem again!

'And you remember her?'

'I kept a photograph,' he admitted. 'I've also seen her in the society columns of *The Times*. She's rarely short of male companions.'

'Do you really think that she and your father were never divorced?'

'It's something I fully intend asking Charles Miller,' he answered quietly. 'I think she's lying. She knows my father's estate will be vast. There've been a couple of times over the years when she's attempted, unsuccessfully, to get back into his good books.'

'She doesn't look as though she needs money now,' said Anna. 'That's a cashmere designer suit she's wearing. Perhaps we're doing her an injustice? Perhaps she *has* come to pay her last respects?'

'I'd like to believe that,' he said, 'but somehow I don't think so.'

Later, as they sat in the vast drawing room waiting for the will to be read, Anna asked quietly, 'What did Charles Miller say about your mother?'

Oliver winced. He'd cornered the solicitor earlier and taken him into his father's study and the news he'd heard hadn't pleased him. 'There was no divorce. My father seemed to think it would serve Rosemary right if she wasn't free to marry anyone else.'

Anna frowned. 'But she could have divorced him, surely? She didn't have to remain married.'

Oliver shrugged. 'I guess they were both playing games.' Rosemary's name had been a taboo subject in the Langford household; instead, Edward had vented his anger on the child she'd left behind.

Anna took Oliver's hand in sympathy, just that and nothing more, yet it created a rush of feeling so intense that it shocked him. How could something as simple as a touch make a mockery of his determination to end their marriage? She'd proved that she was no better than either Rosemary or Melanie. What was wrong with him? Why couldn't he get her out of his system?

When the will was read, the bulk of Edward's estate was naturally left to his son. There were smaller bequests to various relatives, and a modest amount for Melanie. To Anna there was nothing, and to Rosemary there was nothing either—which didn't please Oliver's mother.

The woman's face turned a startling shade of puce and she jumped to her feet. 'I intend to contest the will.' She directed her comments to the solicitor, but they were loud and clear for all to hear. 'Edward and I remained married. He cannot cut me off without a penny.'

'That is your choice,' said Charles gravely, running a finger round the neck of his collar. 'But I have to tell you now, Mrs Langford, that I don't think you'll get very far.'

Oliver took Anna's arm and led her from the drawing room. 'Let's go home. Mrs Hughes will lock up here when everyone's gone.'

It was the way he said home that warmed Anna's heart—it was as though he meant it was her home too. If only. Her six months of marriage had been so full of happiness, so full of love and laughter, that it was difficult to accept it was all over. Perhaps, if she tried very hard, she could pretend for a few more hours that nothing had happened, that they were still deeply in love.

And once inside, when he took off his jacket and tie and unbuttoned his collar, when he flopped down on his favourite armchair in the sitting room, she could almost believe it.

He began to relax, the lines of strain on his face seemed to fade, when suddenly there came a sharp rapping on the door.

Oliver stifled a curse.

'Don't answer it,' said Anna, not wanting to spoil these precious moments.

'It might be Charles, as anxious to escape as I was. I must speak to him.'

But it wasn't Charles' voice Anna could hear as Oliver opened the door—it was Rosemary's, an extremely furious Rosemary.

'Running away is a fool's game,' she shot at her son viciously. 'What's the matter, couldn't you face the thought of me upsetting your precious little tin god of a solicitor?'

'I doubt you'll upset Charles,' he told her calmly.

'Well, he needn't think that I shall sit back and do nothing,' she shrieked. 'I have a right to some of Edward's money.'

'You think what you like,' said Oliver, and Anna was proud of the way he kept his cool. 'It has nothing to do with me.' And she noticed that he didn't invite her in. Not that she could blame him. His mother must be his least favourite person.

'It has a whole lot to do with you,' retorted Rosemary. 'If you were a good son then you'd see me right. I wouldn't need to go through a solicitor. It's going to cost me money to—'

Oliver cut her short. 'I'm sorry but, the way I see it, you gave up the right to being my mother the day you walked out.'

Anna waited with bated breath to hear what Rosemary was going to say next. Perhaps she ought to show her face, give Oliver some support.

But Rosemary had clearly decided she'd said enough. She walked back down the path, turning as she reached the roadway. Anna could see her through the window, her back ramrod straight, her chin high, her lips a slash of angry scarlet in her pale but beautiful face.

'You've not heard the last of this,' she flung icily. 'I shall be around for a while longer. Don't think I'm going to quietly run away; that isn't my style.'

There was more of her in Oliver than he knew, felt Anna. Not only did they resemble each other but they both had the same tenacity of purpose when they thought they were in the right.

When he came back into the room his mouth was set. 'I'm sorry about that.'

And Anna knew that their comfortable togetherness was gone. Oliver was hurting, hurting badly, and she wished there was something she could do to ease his pain.

'Hopefully,' she said soothingly, 'Rosemary will accept that there's no point in fighting this particular battle and will fade gracefully into the background again.'

Oliver crossed to the drinks cupboard, poured himself a large whisky and downed it in one swallow, then poured another before taking it back to his chair. 'Rosemary is one of the world's takers. The only thing she ever gave in her entire life was birth to me. And little good that did her—or me, for that matter.'

Anna frowned. 'What do you mean?'

He shook his head. 'It doesn't matter.' Then he drew in a ragged breath. 'What a day.'

'Funerals are always harrowing occasions.'

'Some more than others,' he growled. 'Come here. I need you.'

His request startled Anna but it didn't enter her head to say no. Instead she moved slowly towards him, locking her eyes into his, ignoring the throb of her pulses, the heat that torched her suddenly sensitive skin, the hammer beats of her heart.

When Oliver pulled her down on to his lap and tucked her head into the hollow of his shoulder, curving an arm about her and holding her close, she felt an echoing beat inside him, a tension he couldn't disguise.

Her heart pounded in excited anticipation. They'd sat like this a hundred times before and always it had led to one thing.

An electric finger stroked her cheek; hot golden eyes watched her mouth as she ran the tip of her tongue over lips that were uncomfortably dry, and quietly he asked, 'When are you going back to Ireland?'

Anna groaned silently. Did he have to talk about such things when she was in a temporary seventh heaven? She didn't want to spoil these precious moments with conversation.

What she really wanted was to slip her hand inside his shirt and feel once again that electrifying hair-roughened skin. She wanted to lift her mouth for a mind-shattering kiss. She wanted—oh, so much.

'Anna?'

She stifled a sigh. 'Tomorrow.' Much too soon if he was going to treat her like this. Much, much too soon. 'But it's only temporary. I'll be moving back to London shortly. Finding myself a job.'

Now shut up and carry on holding me.

For a moment the stroking continued, unsteady fingers moving slowly from her cheek to her throat, brushing back stray strands of hair, pausing thoughtfully on the erratic tell-tale pulse at its base. The tension inside her built into a throbbing inferno.

Then he spoke again. 'Would you be happy in London? I remember you telling me that you were glad to be out of the rat race.' And his fingers moved to touch the swell of one aching breast.

'So I was,' she said in a strangled voice. Dear Lord, did he know what he was doing to her? 'But a girl has to earn a living.'

The wrong thing to have said.

'Or find a rich husband who can feed your fantasies,' he jeered. 'Come to think of it, you're not much different to Rosemary.'

Anna shot off his lap, fury in her eyes now, tension of a different kind zinging through her limbs. 'How dare you? How dare you compare me to that woman?' She was about to say a whole lot more when common sense warned that Oliver had gone through a lot today and perhaps wasn't thinking rationally.

He picked up his drink and took a long, slow sip, watching her through narrowed eyes. 'So you think there's no comparison? Perhaps you ought to look at things from my side of the fence.'

'I think you're tired and you don't know what you're saying.' Anna endeavoured to sound calm, though heaven knew she was furious inside. 'And if the truth's known I'm tired too,' she added with forced quietness. 'I think I'll go up to my room and take a rest.'

Surprisingly he let her go but as she left she heard the clink of bottle on glass. Let him drink himself stupid, she thought. As if I care.

But she did care. She didn't like to see Oliver upset. Burying his father was bad enough but for Rosemary to add to his torment by putting in an appearance and causing a scene was dreadful. And now he'd lashed out at her, and she'd been on the verge of fighting back—which would have created even more problems.

Anna didn't know what time it was when Oliver came to her room. She'd fallen asleep on the bed and in her dream Oliver was chasing her round and round a lake at the dead of night.

Her own screams woke her and Oliver was standing by the bed. It was dark except for the ghostly light from an almost full moon. She wasn't sure whether she was still dreaming. 'Get away from me!' she yelled.

Instead he sat down on the edge of the bed and gathered her to him. 'It's all right,' he said gently, soothingly. 'You were dreaming.'

'I was dreaming about you,' she admitted, more quietly now. 'Actually, it was a nightmare.'

He grimaced at that. 'I guess I said things I shouldn't have.'

'Don't apologise.' Held once more in his arms, Anna felt that she could afford to be magnanimous. Certainly she didn't want to argue—although he wouldn't have said the words if he hadn't thought there was truth in them. He was never, ever, going to accept that her reasons for giving away that money were altruistic. It was futile of her to hope that they might have a future.

As Oliver continued to hold her his eyes glittered, an intensity in their depths that Anna found deeply disturbing. She could feel the heat of his body through the thin silk of his shirt, and the erratic beat of his heart.

There was more to just holding her—he was aroused! The discovery caused her breathing to quicken and she closed her eyes, trying to shut out the sight of this man who was her husband in name only. It wouldn't be wise to let him make love to her, and yet how could she stop him when her need was growing apace with his?

And even though she couldn't see the desire in his eyes she could feel it and smell it. A rampant male. That particular musky smell was Oliver's alone. She'd always claimed it was an aphrodisiac.

And nothing had changed!

# CHAPTER FIVE

WALKING out of Anna's room was sheer torture. Oliver wanted her like he never had before. The way she'd been there for him today, rarely leaving his side—comforting him, even—had triggered emotions he'd thought long since dead.

Physically and spiritually she was all he'd ever wanted in a woman, his ideal mate. But, unfortunately, like the rest of the female sex, her sights were set on other things. Why was it that money always meant so much to a woman?

When Anna had told him off for opening her an account, declaring that he was being too generous, that she could manage on her housekeeping allowance and didn't need any more, he'd believed her. He'd thought how truly wonderful she was, how refreshingly different. It had made him love her all the more.

But she wasn't different at all; she'd just had a different approach. She'd let the money build up into a distinctly healthy amount, which she'd promptly handed over to her ex-lover—if ex was the word.

He might still be her lover for all Oliver knew. Was it something she had plotted from the beginning? She'd said Tony wasn't with her in Ireland but it was mighty suspicious. First the money disappeared and then she did.

Every time he thought about it his blood boiled. He

didn't believe her brother story for one second. Her brother was a successful businessman.

The man in question, according to his father, had been tall and blond and good-looking—and that was how she'd described Tony. It had to be him; it could be no one else. Oliver slammed his bedroom door behind him.

He was glad now that he'd walked out of her room, that he hadn't given in to those insane urges that crept up on him whenever he was alone with her. The trouble was, she was such a vital person. She glowed with energy, her red hair a perfect foil for those sparkling green eyes, and he couldn't resist her. From day one she'd exerted her magic over him.

Admittedly some of the sparkle had dimmed when she turned up for the funeral. Was it the sadness of the occasion or because her source of ready money had dried up? He'd like to bet it was the latter.

Anna packed her bag before she went downstairs, she saw no point in delaying her departure. Oliver, she discovered, had already breakfasted and left.

'Did he leave a message?' she asked as the housekeeper brought in a fresh pot of tea. 'Has he gone to work?' He didn't normally leave this early.

'I've no idea. Would you like scrambled eggs and mushrooms, or bacon and tomato?'

'Just toast, please.'

'Mr Oliver won't like it,' warned Mrs Green with a wag of her finger. 'He gave me strict instructions that you were to eat a good breakfast.'

Then he should have stayed and made sure she did. Anna felt decidedly disgruntled by his absence. He knew she was leaving today. Didn't he want to say goodbye? Had she misinterpreted the signals last night? And what had that slammed door been all about?

She'd thought it was sexual frustration. Obviously she'd been wrong. He didn't want her any more; he'd come to his senses, realised she was the enemy. Well, that was all right with her. When he came back, she'd be gone; he would never see her again. She poured her tea and stirred it so furiously that it spilled into the saucer.

But before Anna had even left the breakfast table Mrs Green announced that she had a visitor.

'It's Rosemary Langford,' she informed Anna through pursed lips. 'I told her Oliver was out but she said she'd like to speak to you. I've put her in the drawing room.'

Anna didn't want to speak to Rosemary—not now, not any time. But there was no getting out of it. 'Very well, Mrs Green. Give me five minutes and then come and rescue me.'

The housekeeper's thin face broke into a smile. 'With pleasure.'

Rosemary wore another black suit in fine wool with a much shorter skirt and high-heeled suede shoes. Anna grudgingly admitted that Rosemary had a good pair of legs for her age. In fact, she was one very smart woman, her jet-black hair brushed severely back this morning and tied in a loose knot in her nape. She most certainly didn't look as though she was in need of a cut of Edward's fortune. And she made Anna feel distinctly underdressed in her cotton shirt and jeans.

The woman had been standing near the window, surveying the autumn tints in the garden. She turned as Anna walked into the room, gold hoop earrings swinging, her smile artificial, her grey eyes wary and calculating. 'So good of you to see me.'

Good didn't enter into it, thought Anna bitterly, she'd had no choice. 'I'm sorry Oliver's not here.'

'It wasn't Oliver I came to see. I want you to speak to him for me, Anna. I want you to persuade him that I should get a share of Edward's money.'

There was nothing like coming straight out with it. Anna wanted to laugh right into the woman's face. 'I'm sorry, I can't do that.'

'Whyever not?'

'Because it has nothing to do with me.'

'Because you've been left out of the will, too? I wonder why that was?' There was a mean gleam in Rosemary's narrowed eyes. 'Did Edward have it in for you, the same as he did me?'

Anna shook her head firmly. There was no way she wanted this woman lumping the two of them together, making out they were both casualties of the will. 'I think my circumstances and yours are miles apart.'

'Oh, I don't know.' Scarlet lips twisted into a meaningful smile. 'I hear your marriage is on the rocks. Your little charade yesterday didn't fool me for one second.'

'And what has that got to do with it?' asked Anna, her eyes flashing, her composure slipping for a second. She'd seen Rosemary latch on to Melanie, seen them looking across at her, so it wasn't hard to guess where she'd got her information from. But she was not going to give the woman the pleasure of knowing how bad the rift was between her and Oliver.

'It means we've both suffered at the hands of the Langford men,' spat Rosemary. 'And, believe me, whether you help or not, I intend fighting for what I believe is rightly mine.'

The gall of the woman was incredible. How could Rosemary even think for one second that she deserved to benefit from Edward's estate? 'Then you'll fight alone,' declared Anna. 'I want no part in it.'

'Actually, I've already begun. I've moved in to Weston Hall.'

The note of triumph in her voice, the toss of her head, the gleam in her eyes, made Anna look at her sharply. 'You're not serious?' In the background the phone rang but it barely registered. This was much more important.

'When I went back there yesterday, everyone was leaving. No one took any notice of me. I simply wandered upstairs and found myself a comfortable bedroom. To think I once thought Edward would lose that magnificent place. I underestimated his business acumen. And it's in even better condition now than it used to be. Is Oliver thinking of moving in?'

'The phone is for you, Anna.' Mrs Green appeared in the doorway.

'Is it Oliver?' Anna prayed it was, she must tell him straight away what Rosemary was doing.

'No, it's the call you were expecting.'

'Oh, yes, I see. Thank you. Rosemary, this may take some time. I think it would be best if you went.'

The woman didn't look bothered; she'd said all

she'd come to say. 'You will pass on the information to Oliver?'

'Naturally.'

'Thank you for seeing me.' And she sailed out with a satisfied smirk on her face.

'Did I do right?' asked the housekeeper. 'You looked mighty worried.'

'Perfect, Mrs Green. Is there anyone on the phone?'

A smile softened the woman's anxious face. 'No. I rang from the other line, the one Oliver had put in his study for when he's sailing the Net.'

Anna grinned. 'I never knew you were so devious. And it's "surfing", Mrs Green.'

'Well, whatever. It did the trick, didn't it?' she asked, her smile even wider.

'Without a doubt. Now I must find Oliver and quickly. Have you really no idea where he is?'

'I've a feeling he planned to see his solicitor,' the housekeeper answered uncertainly.

When Oliver heard the news he was livid, and in no time Anna saw his car shoot straight past Weston Lodge and up to the main house, skidding round the corner as he went. She hoped he hadn't driven like that all the way from Cambridge.

It was a good hour before he returned. Anna had waited impatiently and met him at the door. Her heart went out to him when she saw the deep lines etched into his brow, the distress in his eyes. She wanted to comfort him, hold him—take him to bed. This last thought shocked her. Where had that come from?

'I'm sorry she dragged you into it,' he said. 'I've managed to get rid of her—for the time being.'

'Do you think she'll stay around while she's contesting the will?' asked Anna in concern. 'Where does she actually live?'

'I've no idea on both counts,' he answered shortly. 'And I can't say that I'm interested. I could murder a coffee, though. Ask Mrs G, will you, while I get changed?'

Ten minutes later, the pin-striped suit replaced by black jeans and a thin crew-neck sweater, a mug of coffee cradled between his palms, Oliver sat looking at her. 'Who'd have thought things would turn out like this.'

'What did Charles have to say?' Anna's coffee was on the table at her side, her hands folded neatly on her lap. She sat still and calm but inwardly she was furious over Rosemary's behaviour. Oliver's mother had no right doing this to him.

'That she hasn't a leg to stand on. But I don't think that's going to stop her. She's set her mind on getting something out of this. She does the same with every man in her life, and there have been many. I've done some digging. I really don't like what I've found out,' he added grimly.

Anna didn't feel she could ask for details; it was no longer any of her business. 'Are you going to live up at the Hall yourself?'

'Not on your life.' His answer was quick in coming and very definite. 'I'll never live there. I'm putting it on the market—this house as well.'

Anna stopped in the act of picking up her coffee

cup. 'But Weston Hall's been in your family for generations, Oliver. How can you do that?'

He shrugged unconcernedly. 'Home can be the humblest cottage. That place is a pile of bricks and mortar, far too big for me. I don't know why my father carried on living there.'

'Have you told Rosemary?'

'No. She'd be back in there like a thief in the night, taking everything she could lay her hands on. She thinks I'm moving in and hopefully she won't find out any differently until it's too late.'

Anna finally drank her now almost cold coffee. 'It will be a mammoth task sorting everything. I could help, if you like?' Her heart pitter-pattered as she made the offer. Quite why she'd done it, she wasn't sure. It had come from deep within her.

Oliver's eyes narrowed. 'I thought you were leaving?'

'I don't have to,' she said with a faint smile and a lift of her slender shoulders. 'And with Rosemary possibly still lurking I thought maybe you could do with some support?'

Oliver looked at her for a long suspended moment. Anna felt a faint eruption inside her, a quivering response to the query in those golden eyes.

No! That wasn't the reason she'd offered, she told herself firmly. She felt sorry for him, that was all.

'Well, thank you, Anna, that's kind of you.' But a raised brow suggested that he wasn't altogether sure of her motives.

'It's not because I'm hoping to get anything out of it,' she pointed out swiftly and firmly. 'I'm doing it solely to help you.'

'Why would you want to do that?' And still the golden eyes watched her.

Desire began to pump, sensual liquid desire that found its way into every vein and every nerve, heightening her awareness, warming her skin. 'Because,' she said slowly, 'I'm not entirely insensitive to your needs. Maybe our marriage didn't work out, but it doesn't mean to say I hate you, or wouldn't do anything to help you.'

'And what needs would those be?' His voice deepened, his eyes burning into hers in such a way that she felt sure he knew her every thought, her every emotion.

She drew in a deep, steadying breath. 'It will take many weeks to sort through your father's stuff, to decide what to get rid of and what to keep.'

'And you're prepared to live here with me while all of this goes on? Without asking for anything in return?' He paused long enough to let his question sink in, and then added bitterly, 'In my experience, no woman does anything for nothing.'

In other words, he still didn't trust her. He probably thought she'd bag the family silver while he wasn't looking. 'If that's what you think,' she snapped, her eyes a vivid flash of emerald in a pale, distraught face, 'then forget I offered. I'll go and tell Mrs Green I won't be here for lunch. I have a plane to catch.' Her head was high as she pushed herself out of the chair.

But before she reached the door, Oliver leapt up and laid a hand on her shoulder. 'No, Anna, don't leave. I'm sorry; I'm touched by your offer. You took me by surprise, that's all.' He smiled wryly. 'I would like your help.'

His smile did something to her—melted her anger, made her smile back in return. 'I promise you won't be disappointed.'

And nor was he. In the days that followed, Oliver truly enjoyed having Anna around. There was an enormous amount of work to be done, much more than he'd first thought, and they worked steadily side by side, hour after hour, day after day.

They separated everything into various categories. Some to be kept for his own personal use, although there wasn't much of that—he wanted no reminders. Stuff to be dumped, some to go to charity, and the rest to either be sold separately or with the house.

And the more time they spent together, the more difficult he found it to remain detached. His feelings for Anna had not faded one little bit. She'd let him down, she'd disappointed him, she'd angered him— made him furious, in fact—but working beside that delectable body day after day soon began to tell on him.

He couldn't sleep at night for thinking about her, wondering whether he dared go to her room. What would happen if he did? If he took her into his bed now, she would think he'd forgiven her, would believe there was hope—whereas he still wasn't sure that he trusted her motives. He wanted to, he really did, but past experience had taught him that it was safest to let his head rule his heart.

But all his good intentions went by the board one morning when she tripped over the flex of a lamp and fell against him. It was like a replay of the day they'd first met. His arms instinctively went around her and the same sensual perfume had the same drugging effect.

With a groan, his arms tightened and everything he'd held in check came pulsing uncontrollably to life. The feel of her tempting, exciting body burst open the floodgates of desire.

And when she didn't resist, when he felt her tremble, when he saw the difficulty she had in breathing, he knew that he was not going to let her go.

He cupped her face between his palms, looked for several haunting, meaningful seconds into her incredible luminous eyes, and with a further agonised groan his mouth closed over hers.

Anna was beyond stopping him. She was amazingly helpless. His lips burned where they touched. It had been so long since he'd kissed her, really kissed her, that her limbs had gone fluid and if he dared let her go she feared that she would melt into a pool on the floor.

'Oh, Anna!' he breathed. 'What you do to me.' And his tongue darted between her lips, seeking and finding the pleasure he desperately desired.

It was Anna's turn to moan, to feel a need so deep that it scared her. Her tongue played games with his; she tasted the never-to-be-forgotten maleness of him, ground her hips against his, felt the damning evidence of his arousal.

More excitement, more fear. She ought to stop him but how could she? How could she deny herself such exquisite pleasure? It had been inevitable from the moment she offered to stay that something like this would happen. The surprising part was that it had taken so long.

All the emotions she'd kept bottled up rushed to the surface. She returned kiss for earth-shattering kiss, deeply, wantonly, and when he picked her up and carried her effortlessly towards the stairs she did nothing to stop him.

Her body needed his; it needed to be loved, it begged fulfilment. Neither of them spoke, tension building, breathing becoming difficult, painful even, and in the bedroom—she assumed the one Oliver had used when he was staying with his father—he dropped her on to the bed and raced to get out of his clothes.

Anna watched with fascination the frenzy that was driving him. The burning desire, the jerky movements as first shirt and then shoes and socks were ripped off. Belt, zip, and he almost tripped in his haste to get out of his trousers.

Her stomach tightened when a pair of black briefs was all that was left between him and his modesty. And there was nothing very modest about what they were hiding.

It was time to get undressed herself. She'd lain almost trance-like as she watched Oliver's frantic actions, but now her hunger got the better of her. Consumed by fire, pulses racing, heart thudding, her breasts already aching for his touch, she leapt off the bed and began to lift her sweater.

'No! Don't! That's my job.' His urgent voice reached into her unconscious.

She hadn't even realised that he was watching her. His briefs were gone. He stood tall and totally male in front of her, perfectly at ease with his nakedness. 'This is all right, Anna?' he asked quietly, almost anxiously.

No words would come so she swallowed hard and nodded instead. He took the bottom of her lambswool sweater. She raised her arms and he stripped it off in one fluid movement. Her jeans followed with not quite so much patience.

His breathing was ragged and Anna felt his tremors as he unclipped her bra and tossed it across the room, quickly followed by the matching black lacy briefs.

They fell on each other then, and Anna felt herself land with a thud on the bed. Oliver sucked first one and then the other burning nipple into his eager mouth, while his hand explored and tortured other regions.

Anna writhed beneath him, her hand seeking and finding what she wanted most.

'Don't touch,' he groaned, 'or I promise you I'll never make it.'

But he did make it, and as he entered her, as their bodies fused, as passion took over, he wondered how he was going to live without her. And as they lay in throbbing silence afterwards, their limbs too heavy to move, their hearts slowly getting back to normal, Oliver knew that this had been the best time ever— and, judging by Anna's wild climactic response, the best for her, too.

It wasn't until she cuddled into the crook of his arm, making little cooing sounds of satisfaction, stroking her fingers over his sweat-slicked chest, that it occurred to him that maybe this was what had been behind her offer of help. Maybe this had been in her mind all along—maybe she'd seen it as a way of getting through to him, of getting their marriage back on track.

So that she could wheedle even more money out of him!

His blood ran cold.

# CHAPTER SIX

ANNA couldn't sleep. She lay in bed and watched a silver crescent of moon move slowly across the velvet darkness of the sky. She had thought, mistakenly as it turned out, that after their fantastic lovemaking Oliver would suggest she move back in to his bed. She had stupidly hoped it was the beginning of a reconciliation.

She could still feel the touch of his hands and mouth on her body, still feel a churning in her stomach, a pulsing through her veins. She clenched her thighs tightly together, nursing the sensation at their apex. How could Oliver do this to her? How could he leave her in limbo like this?

After their fast and furious enjoyment of each other's bodies, they'd gone back to their sorting and packing, but the atmosphere between them had changed. It had become charged with electric tension, she was far too aware of him to concentrate on her task.

All she'd wanted to do was feast her eyes on him. She'd wanted to touch, to share, to feel, to continue this unexpected togetherness. But Oliver, sadly, seemed to regret his actions, beginning work with renewed vigour, practically ignoring her, not stopping until it was time for them to go back home to the meal Mrs Green always had ready for them.

After they'd eaten, he shut himself in his study to

read his emails and check on the days running of his business. His computer was networked to his various branches and he'd explained to Anna that without it he would not have been able to take so much time off work.

He finally surfaced at half past ten and there were deep lines of strain etched into his face. 'I'm going to bed,' he announced abruptly.

Anna had been reading a book while she waited for him, and now she looked up in disappointment. 'Don't you even want a drink?'

'No, nothing.' But the look he gave her didn't suggest nothing. It suggested he'd like to make love to her again and a quick heat invaded her limbs. She wanted to say, I'll come to bed with you, but she knew that the suggestion had to come from him.

It didn't. He'd gone straight to his room, and here she was unable to sleep for thinking about Oliver, thinking what it would be like to share his bed again, to have him make crazy, passionate love to her every night, the way he used to.

He had proved this afternoon that he found it hard to resist her, so why was he ignoring her now? Did he deeply regret what had happened? Was he castigating himself? Was he still of the opinion that she was after his money?

It was going to be difficult working together with sexual tension like this sparking between them. Had he thought of that when he let his male urges get the better of him? If it was to be an on-off thing, she would rather it had never happened—in fact, she wouldn't have gone along with it had she known.

Anna was down to breakfast before Oliver, and

when he joined her his shadowed eyes suggested that he hadn't slept much either.

And when they got to the house he carefully busied himself in a separate room. He was making it very obvious that there was going to be no repeat of what had happened yesterday.

When, a short time later, she heard a sound behind her Anna couldn't stop her heart skipping several beats. It did it automatically whenever he was near. She whirled around with a smile on her face, but her smile faded and her heart crashed dangerously when she saw who stood there.

'What are you doing here?' asked Melanie, her blue eyes coldly questioning. 'Where's Oliver?'

'He's around,' Anna told her calmly. 'I'm helping him sort his father's stuff.'

'And what gives you that right?' she demanded haughtily. 'I thought you only came for Uncle Edward's funeral. Why are you still here? I sincerely hope you're not trying to worm your way back into Oliver's life, because it won't work. Oliver doesn't love you any more—if he ever did.'

'I think what Oliver and I do is none of your business,' retorted Anna, straightening her back and eyeing Melanie coldly. She was relieved when Oliver chose that moment to come into the room because she didn't relish this type of conversation. She wasn't up to discussing her husband with his ex-girlfriend. Or was it current girlfriend? She suddenly wasn't sure.

When Melanie flung herself into his arms and lifted her face expectantly to his, and when Oliver obediently kissed her, a stab of jealousy pierced the shat-

tered pieces of Anna's heart. She couldn't bear to see
them together, especially as less than twenty-four
hours earlier he'd been making love to her.

Why had she given herself so eagerly? she asked
herself. Why hadn't she remembered Melanie? Why
had she let her feelings run away with her? Why
hadn't she been stronger?

The brief kiss over, Melanie pouted delicately.
'You should have asked me to help you, Oliver. I had
no idea you were getting rid of any of Uncle
Edward's things. In fact, I can't see the point unless—' she frowned '—you're planning to buy yourself a whole heap of new stuff. Rosemary said that—'

'Rosemary?' he interrupted harshly. 'She's still
hanging around?'

Anna saw the way his eyes narrowed suspiciously,
the way his body froze.

'I don't know what you mean hanging around. But
I did see her the other day,' Melanie admitted.

'She's staying locally?'

'In Cambridge, I believe,' she answered. 'Why, is
it important?'

'Which hotel?' he snapped, not bothering to answer
her question.

'I don't know, but we're having lunch together tomorrow. I could—'

'No need; I have nothing to say to her.' But the
grimness of his jaw suggested quite the opposite.

Melanie shrugged her narrow shoulders. 'She's still
pretty worked up about the will.'

'Is that what she said? Has she asked you to put in
a good word for her?'

'Of course not,' said Melanie. 'Don't fret yourself, Oliver.'

He turned away impatiently. 'Anna, how about some coffee?'

He was asking *her* to make coffee for him and Melanie! It was like asking her to accept that they were lovers. Anna wanted to refuse but what good would it do her? Her face was darkly furious, though, as she left the room, and all the while she was out she kept picturing the two of them together.

And her misgivings were justfied when she returned and found them sitting on the leather chesterfield. Oliver's arm was about Melanie's shoulders and she looked as though she'd been crying. But when she looked at Anna there was a light of triumph in her eyes and it wasn't hard to see that they'd been crocodile tears.

'Here we are.' Anna tried to sound cheerful as she put the tray on the table, but it was all she could do to pour Melanie's coffee and hand it to her civilly.

And when Oliver announced that he was taking Melanie out for lunch and probably wouldn't be back, she gave an inward groan of despair. 'She's very upset over my father,' he explained. 'Coming here has brought back memories.'

I bet, thought Anna. Memories of what she'd once had with Oliver, what she wanted again, what she was going out of her way to get.

'There's no need for you to stay, either,' he said, with a note of concern. 'You deserve some time to yourself, you've been working hard.'

As far as Anna was concerned, it wasn't work. It had been pleasure simply being in Oliver's company.

She'd begun to hope for something more from their relationship; she'd begun to think they were mending bridges that had once seemed beyond repair, especially after yesterday.

But Melanie had swiftly put paid to that—and, if Melanie was to be believed, she'd been looking after his needs anyway. Perhaps the reason for Oliver making love to her was frustration because the blonde hadn't been around. He'd been using her as a substitute.

The thought was like a solid punch in the stomach; it almost had her doubling over with pain. 'Thank you, but I think I'll stay,' she said tightly. 'I have nothing else to do.'

'No, you can't do that,' protested Melanie with surprising vehemence. 'You need to take time off as well. You know what they say about all work and no play.'

Anna glanced at Oliver and saw him nodding his agreement. Did that mean he thought she was dull? There had certainly been no dullness about their love-making yesterday. She had responded uninhibitedly—she'd had no choice—it had been like instantaneous combustion. She'd had no control over her actions. And nor had he.

So what game was he playing?

'I might. I'll see,' she said.

'You really ought to make some time for yourself,' declared Melanie firmly.

'My sentiments entirely,' added Oliver.

When they had gone, Anna found that she didn't want to stay after all. She wandered up to the bedroom they'd used but simply looking at the still crumpled sheets aroused a torrent of anger.

All that had driven him had been need. He'd used her. She ought to have realised that last night when he didn't even kiss her before he went to bed. She smoothed the sheets automatically, resolving never to let herself get into this situation again.

She returned to Weston Lodge but it was Mrs Green's day off and she didn't feel like making herself any lunch so she decided it was time to pay her parents a visit—until she remembered that she didn't have her car, that it was still sitting outside the cottage in Ireland.

Her parents lived in the depths of the countryside on the other side of Cambridge, not even on a bus route. A taxi would be horrendously expensive, so what other course did it leave her?

There was Edward's car, of course, tucked in its garage up at the Hall—his Land Rover, too. Why not take one of those? Oliver had said he was going to sell them but he'd done nothing yet and she felt sure he wouldn't mind. He'd left the keys to the Hall with her and she'd seen the car keys hanging up in the kitchen.

In the end she took the Land Rover, feeling that the Rolls was a little too much for her, but when she got to her parents' they weren't in and she cursed her stupidity. She ought to have phoned. Mindless going all that way on the spur of the moment.

It wasn't her day, she decided. She'd try her brother, and if he wasn't at his office then she'd—what would she do? Lunch somewhere alone? Go to the cinema? Do what? It was amazing how lost she felt.

During the last few days she'd come to rely on Oliver's presence, had almost begun to feel secure— in his friendship, if nothing more. Now she wasn't so sure. Melanie had only to lift her finger and he'd gone running. What did that tell her?

She shook her head to try and clear it of such unwanted thoughts and headed back towards Cambridge.

Chris was in and pleased to see her. 'I thought you were still in Ireland. I'm about to have a late lunch. Do you want to join me or have you eaten?'

'It's what I was banking on,' she said, giving her brother an extra big hug.

'Hey, what's that for? Do I sense a need to talk? Is all well with you and Oliver?'

Anna grimaced, she hadn't realised that she was giving herself away. 'I'll tell you over lunch.'

. And she told him the whole sorry story.

'Oh, Lord,' he exclaimed. 'I never realised it would cause this much trouble.' Chris put down his knife and fork and looked at her anxiously. 'You have told him what the money was for?'

Anna shook her head.

'Why not? Heavens, Anna, you can't put your marriage in jeopardy because of me.' He shook his head, his navy eyes worried.

'He wouldn't listen,' Anna admitted sadly. 'He thought the worst. And dammit, Chris, if he can think that of his own wife then it doesn't say much for the state of our marriage, does it? I thought trust came into these things. Huh!' she exclaimed contemptuously. 'He doesn't trust me any further than he can throw me. Besides, his old girlfriend's back in his life.'

Anna hadn't realised exactly how much she was giving away until her brother put his hand on hers across the table. 'Calm down, sis,' he said anxiously. 'I'm sure you must be mistaken. Dawn said she'd never seen a man so much in love as Oliver.'

'Maybe Oliver was, but Oliver's not any more,' she retorted bitterly.

'You're sure of that?'

'Positive.'

'I still think you should tell him. I've had a part payment; I'm back on track and I'll soon be able to repay the money.'

'It's not the point, Chris.' But how she wished her brother had never asked for help in the first place. It would have saved her so much heartache. On the other hand, it was best she'd found out what Oliver was like sooner rather than later.

She'd heard of girls who had control freaks as husbands, men who demanded to know where every penny was spent, what they'd been doing with their time and who with. Wanting to run their lives for them. Was Oliver like that? Was this the tip of the iceberg? Would things have got worse? Was she well rid of him?

'I think it's entirely the point,' insisted her brother. 'You're as unhappy as hell. You've changed since I last saw you. You were so vibrant—now look at you. You look like death warmed up. Do Mum and Dad know your marriage is on the rocks?'

'No,' she answered with a wry grimace. 'I've just been over there, actually, but they were out.'

'It will gut them.'

'I know,' she said with a heavy sigh. 'It's why I've kept quiet.'

'You mean you were hoping it would blow over, that you might get back together?'

'Something like that.'

'He's an idiot if he lets you go.'

'Maybe Oliver never loved me,' she said ruefully. 'His father said he married me on the rebound, I'm beginning to think he was right.'

'So why did he finish with this other woman?'

Anna's eyes flashed. 'The money thing again.'

Chris's breath hissed out loudly and he shook his head. 'The man has a complex. No wonder you're confused. Do you still love him?'

Anna lifted her slender shoulders. 'I don't know.'

'Which means you do. I think you should give him one more chance. Tell him about me, tell him I asked you to keep it a secret, and if that doesn't work then…' He spread his hands expansively. 'Then send him to me. I'll make him see sense.'

'But don't you see, Chris? I don't want him back on those terms. He should never have doubted me in the first place.'

'I agree. I've met the most wonderful girl in the world and I'd trust her with my life. I really would. I guess that's true love.'

'Oh, Chris.' Anna's eyes opened wide. 'You must have been dying to tell me and I've been rabbiting on about my own woes. I'm sorry. What's her name and where did you meet her? Tell me everything.'

*     *     *

When Anna eventually got home Oliver was waiting for her. His eyes were hard and cold, his whole body as taut as a violin string. 'Where the hell have you been?'

Anna frowned as she felt a cold shiver run down her spine. The words 'control freak' sprang to mind. 'What does it matter to you?'

'I see you took my father's Land Rover.'

'So that's the issue, is it?' she asked with lifted brows. 'I was supposed to have asked permission.'

'Now you're being ridiculous,' he snapped. 'You did say you might stay on at the Hall, I couldn't find you, I was worried.'

Oliver worried! That was a laugh. 'I'm sorry, but there was no one to ask,' she tossed coolly. 'I've been prisoner here long enough; I thought it was time I went out.'

'Prisoner?' His brows curved into a disbelieving arc.

'In that I don't have my car.'

'I see. I can't recall you saying that it was an in-convenience.'

And it hadn't been, up until now, but she wasn't going to tell him that. 'I decided to visit my parents. Do you have a problem with that?'

Oliver's eyes narrowed. 'How are they?'

Anna shrugged. 'Actually, they weren't in. So I had lunch with Chris instead.'

'The phantom brother?'

Anna didn't like the sarcasm in his voice and her eyes flashed. 'The very same.'

'When am I going to meet him?'

'I think never, considering our marriage is over,'

she retorted sharply and angrily. She had thought on
the way home that perhaps Chris was right and she
ought to make Oliver listen to the truth. But his attitude now made her swiftly change her mind. He
wouldn't believe her if she wrote it in blood.

'That's a pity. I think Chris and I would have had
plenty to talk about.'

'Like whether I gave the money to him or Tony,
is that what you mean?' she asked caustically, while
trying to ignore her fierce swell of unbidden desire.

What was it about Oliver that whenever they ar-
gued she felt this insane urge to make love to him?
It always happened. Was it the fire in his eyes, the
slow burn in his cheeks, the tautness of his body?
Whatever, it was doing things to her that shouldn't
be allowed to happen, not any longer.

'Mmm, Tony,' he said thoughtfully. 'Have you
seen him recently?'

Her eyes shot sparks of fierce anger. 'You know
damn well I haven't. I've been nowhere since I got
here.'

His look was disbelieving but for some reason he
didn't press the issue. Instead, he said, 'Maybe you
should keep the Land Rover as a runaround. I hadn't
realised that you felt tied. Why didn't you take the
Roller? It would have created much more of an impression.'

'For whom? There's no one I want to impress,
Oliver.' She'd had enough of this conversation. 'How
did your lunch with Melanie go?'

He smiled for the first time since she'd got home
and Anna felt swift daggers of jealousy. She tried to
tell herself that she couldn't possibly be jealous when

she wasn't in love with Oliver any more, but it made no difference. She was jealous. The green-eyed monster reared its head every time she thought about Oliver and Melanie together.

'We went to The Riverside. They serve excellent food and—'

'Yes, I know. You used to take me there,' she cut in shortly. They had agreed it was their special place—and now he'd taken Melanie. How cruel could he get?

'So I did,' he said, with a self-conscious laugh as though he'd just remembered.

'So where is she now? I expected you to spend the rest of the day with her.'

'She had other plans.'

Anna thought he sounded disappointed. 'Have you mended your differences? Are you two an item again?'

'Why do you ask?' Dark brows rode high. 'Does it bother you?'

'Not in the least,' she lied. 'I'm only mildly curious. You don't have to tell me.'

Nor did he, which piqued her beyond measure.

Mrs Green had prepared everything for their supper; all Anna had to do was grill the chicken breasts and toss the salad. Oliver shut himself in his study and told her to give him a call when it was ready.

She was unprepared, therefore, when she turned around from the sink and found him watching her. Her hand flew subconsciously to her throat. 'You gave me a fright. How long have you been there?' For a fraction of a second she'd seen a gleam in those golden eyes, gone in an instant, possibly imagined, but it nevertheless made her jittery inside.

'Long enough to know that you'd look even better in that overall if you wore nothing underneath.'

Anna had donned one of Mrs Green's tabards to protect her silk blouse and she had a quick mental image of herself in that alone. It would cover front and back—but from the side…?

She felt herself blushing furiously. She didn't want Oliver thinking this way about her, not now he was friendly with Melanie again. What was he trying to do, play one off against the other? And for what reason?

'I thought you were working.'

'I couldn't concentrate.'

Because he was thinking about Melanie? Wondering who it was she had gone off to see? But if she was planning to use her again in the other girl's absence, then he was in for a big disappointment. She wasn't going to make the same mistake twice.

Except that her insides had already begun to sizzle at the mere thought of him touching her, of his hands sliding beneath the tabard and touching her breasts which had peaked beneath the thin silk.

'Supper won't be long,' she said coolly, surprising herself by the steadiness of her voice. 'If you want to go and pour yourself a drink and relax while you're waiting…'

'Good idea. G&T for you?'

'I don't think so.' She needed a clear head to get through the next hour or so; she had to be on her guard lest she weaken and let him slip through her defences the way he had yesterday.

She was still puzzled as to why he had made love to her so wonderfully one minute and then virtually ignored her the next. Admittedly, they'd always been good in bed together; it had been a dream part of their marriage, perhaps the best part. Perhaps that was all they'd had—a sexual attraction which they'd mistaken for love. And perhaps he still was sexually attracted to her, and sometimes he fought it, sometimes he didn't.

Oliver returned bearing two tall crystal glasses chinking with ice and a slice of lemon. 'I don't like drinking alone.'

She had to admit that the gin and tonic was both delicious and refreshing. The heat in the kitchen wasn't entirely due to the cooker and she swallowed her drink more quickly than was wise, making her head feel fuzzy and her mind not quite as sharp as it had been a few minutes ago.

'Another one?' Oliver was only halfway through his.

'No, thank you.'

'Shall I open a bottle of wine to go with our meal?'

She looked at him sharply. 'What is this? Are you trying to get me drunk?'

'Perish the thought,' he said with a flicker of a smile. 'I like my women to know what they're doing.'

My women! How many did he have? Were there others besides herself and Melanie? Or was it a figure of speech and she was overreacting? She guessed the latter—hoped it was the latter. 'I prefer to be in control of myself as well,' she said primly.

'Except that you don't always manage it.'

He lifted a knowing brow and Anna's cheeks

flushed again. Did he have to remind her how easily she gave way to desire? But it was only with him, never anyone else—didn't he know that? Tony hadn't aroused her even half as much as Oliver did—as Oliver used to, she corrected herself quickly.

'Don't be embarrassed, it's one of the things I like most about you.'

'Still?' she asked, managing to inject a note of scepticism into her voice.

'Some things never go away, Anna.' There was a deep suggestiveness in his tone that had her looking at him quickly. But his face was impassive. 'Like the smell of burning. It takes ages for it to—'

With a shriek Anna turned to the grill and pulled out the charred remains of the chicken. How could she have let him distract her to this extent?

'It's your fault,' she exclaimed crossly. 'Why couldn't you have kept out of the way?'

'You look delightful when you're angry.'

She groaned inwardly wishing he wouldn't play up to her like this.

'You won't think I'm delightful if I throw it all over you,' she declared fiercely. 'You'd best get out while I dispose of the mess.'

'Why don't you let me do it?' He put down his glass and took a step towards her.

But Anna didn't want him interfering; she wanted him out. 'No! Just go, will you?' She was overreacting again but she couldn't help it. He'd worked her up into such a state that if he came any nearer she would explode.

But he did come nearer. And he tried to take the

grillpan out of her hand, and when she resisted the two pieces of burnt chicken skidded to the floor.

'Now look what you've done,' she yelled, and to her dismay she burst into tears.

# CHAPTER SEVEN

OLIVER was horrified to see Anna crying.

He hated any woman to cry. It made him feel helpless. Should he console her or do as she'd asked and get out of the way? Sanity said he should go; instinct made him take the pan off her and pull her into his arms.

'It's not the end of the world,' he said soothingly. 'We'll eat out. It's not a problem.'

'Where? The Riverside?' she snapped.

He winced as she drove home the mistake he'd made in taking Melanie there. It had been Melanie's idea and he hadn't been thinking straight. All he'd known was that he'd been tormented ever since he'd lost his head and made love to Anna.

It had made him crave more, crave the life they'd once had, but his marriage had gone badly wrong. And so he'd grasped Melanie's suggestion as the diversion he so badly needed.

Melanie was devastated by Edward's death—she'd loved her godfather dearly—and despite her faults Oliver felt he couldn't completely abandon her at this critical time. But he hadn't enjoyed himself and he had in fact been relieved when Melanie announced that she had somewhere else to go.

When he got home and found Anna missing, he'd gone crazy. He'd been so looking forward to spending more time with her, even though he knew it would torture his soul.

What he'd really wanted to do when she did return was sweep her up in his arms and kiss her senseless. But he knew that would solve nothing, so he'd conjured up his anger in order to distance himself from her—and had succeeded for a short time.

But in his study, he'd been unable to concentrate. All he could see on the computer screen was Anna's gorgeous face, those wonderfully alive eyes, that flamboyant hair, the wide, infinitely kissable mouth.

It had forced him to find her and he'd stood in the kitchen doorway for a good couple of minutes before she spotted him. His fantasy of seeing her in the bright yellow tabard and nothing else almost had him pouncing on her and ripping her clothes off. Maybe if she hadn't turned when she did he would have done.

Even now, holding her, soothing her, there was nothing calm about the parts of him that she couldn't see. He felt tortured by fire, by a need so intense it was painful. 'We can go wherever you like.' Bed, preferably.

'I'm not hungry.'

Nor was he—except for love. Or was it lust? He hated that word and yet he knew deep down inside that it was lust that drove him, that had always driven him where Anna was concerned. He'd committed the cardinal crime of letting his heart rule his head when he'd asked her to marry him. Not even his heart. It was the bit between his legs that was the problem.

His father had done the same thing with Rosemary. He'd been besotted by a pretty face and a nice pair of legs and look where that had got him. No wonder Edward had been appalled when he saw his son making exactly the same mistake.

'You need to eat,' he told Anna firmly. 'You've lost weight; you can't afford to lose any more.' And still he held her, and still his damned male hormones played riot.

'As if that matters to you.' Anna finally tried to struggle free.

But he needed to hold her, he needed to feel her exciting body against him. He needed to dream a little longer. 'I care whether you're looking after yourself,' he said gruffly, forcing the words past a choking knot in his throat.

'I can't think why,' she retorted.

That hurt, her thinking that he didn't care any longer. He supposed he deserved it, considering he'd walked out on her. It had been a bad move, but he'd needed time to think about what she'd done. Before he'd reached any decisions, though, she'd upped and left—and he hadn't a clue where she'd gone. The discovery had left him stunned.

He'd wanted to look for her immediately but his father had persuaded him that to do so would create more problems in the future. 'Women only ever want what they can get out of a man,' Edward had said firmly. 'They never change. They might promise you the earth, you might even think for a little while that they've changed, but it never lasts. They're like leopards.'

And so Oliver had bowed to his father's wisdom. It hadn't stopped him from ringing Dawn and persuading her to tell him where Anna was, and maybe if Melanie hadn't revealed the same flaw in her nature then he might have gone after her, it had made him think twice and then three times and then four, and in the end he had convinced himself that he'd done the right thing.

'If you don't want to go out, Anna—' he lifted her chin so that he could look into her face '—then at least let me do us something to eat.' The tears were gone but her eyes were still pink-rimmed. Lord, how he wanted to bed her. 'What were we having with the chicken?' he asked, wondering how he managed to keep the longing out of his voice.

'Salad,' she answered thinly, 'and potatoes.'

'So how about I make us a potato omelette to go with the salad?' he asked, deliberately cheerful. 'You run along and freshen up, and I'll sort everything out here.'

He was afraid she'd refuse, that she'd race up to her bedroom and stay there for the rest of the evening. But finally she heaved a sigh and gave him a weak, tremulous smile. 'OK.'

When she came back down Anna had changed into a rust-coloured all-in-one trouser suit. It fastened with a zip down the front and he wondered if she knew how tempting that zip was.

At first glance, the suit looked demure and safe with its high neck and short sleeves. It was probably the reason she'd worn it. But that zip! He couldn't take his eyes off it.

Oliver imagined himself pulling it down and revealing slow inch by slow inch her delicately scented skin, skin so pale and soft and smooth that it excited him just to touch it. And the thought of exposing those perfectly rounded breasts which fit so beautifully into his palms caused an ache deep in his groin.

He groaned—he couldn't help himself—and Anna looked at him with a swift frown. 'Is something wrong?'

Everything! Don't you know that? From somewhere, he managed to drag up a wry smile, and he patted his stomach. 'Excuse me, I'm hungry.' He wasn't so sure she believed it was a grumble of hunger, though.

'I thought we'd eat in here,' he said. 'Less trouble.' And less chance of intimacy. There were no cosy seats to relax in afterwards, just two kitchen stools and a granite breakfast bar.

But it was still a mistake. The seats didn't have to be comfortable, there didn't have to be candles and music—the very fact that he was sitting next to Anna was enough. They could have been anywhere, in an igloo in the frozen wastes of Siberia or in the most romantic of restaurants in the most romantic place in the world and it would have been the same.

He should never have insisted they eat together. He should have gone out; he shouldn't have come back. How was he going to get through the rest of the evening without giving way to the ferocious desire that was twisting him into knots?

'Nice omelette,' she said. 'Your cooking skills have improved.'

He knew she was referring to a disastrous meal he had cooked them early on in their marriage. It wasn't that he was a bad cook—he'd always liked to cook for himself whenever Mrs G let him anywhere near the kitchen. But on that particular day—when he'd wanted so much to impress Anna—everything had gone wrong.

From the overdone pheasant to the collapsed soufflé. Anna had gallantly eaten everything he'd put in front of her, but they'd ended up in fits of laughter. One thing had led to another, kisses had led to making love on the dining room floor, and it was yet another fantastic memory to add to his store. 'That was a day I shall never forget,' he admitted.

Anna stilled for a fraction of a second.

'I've never cooked soufflé again, or eaten pheasant,' he admitted.

'It wasn't a complete disaster.'

It was his turn to stop breathing.

Was she referring to them making love?

'I'd have probably ended up in tears if it had happened to me,' she said, 'whereas you simply laughed.'

And was that all she remembered? 'You laughed at me first,' he reminded her.

'Because you looked so stricken. I had to do something to lighten the moment.'

'How about some of that laughter now?' He hadn't meant to say that; he didn't want her to think that he intended the day to end the same as that other one had. 'I mean, I'm sorry if I laid into you earlier. I seem to make a habit of ruining things.'

'It's all right,' she said with a vague shrug and an even vaguer smile.

'No, it's not all right,' he said, bouncing his palms off the worktop to give emphasis to his words. 'I shouldn't have yelled at you for going out. I'd not given a thought to the fact that you had no transport. I'm sorry, Anna.'

'You're forgiven,' she said demurely. 'Finish your omelette before it goes cold.'

But he was the one who didn't feel like eating now. Sitting so close that their elbows occasionally touched, so close that if he opened his legs just that little bit wider his thigh would brush hers, was doing dangerous things to him.

With an effort, he turned the conversation to everyday subjects, and they both managed to finish their meal. 'Would you like another gin?' he asked as he put down his knife and fork.

Anna shook her head. 'I'd prefer a coffee.'

'You're not turning teetotal on me?'

'You know I don't drink much.'

'But another one won't hurt. Come on, Anna. Let's relax at the end of a wearing day.'

'It hasn't been wearing for me,' she said. 'In fact, it was quite relaxing until…'

She'd come home and he'd given her a third degree. He felt suitably chastised. 'In that case, you make your coffee while I mix my drink.' He left the kitchen gasping for air. It was stupid, he knew. This was the woman he was going to divorce. What right had she to make him feel like this?

That's right, lay the blame on Anna, accused his conscience. She hasn't done anything; it's all in your mind. A mind which was as filled with confusion as the endless wires in a telephone junction box.

When he returned to the kitchen, Anna had stacked the dishes in the dishwasher, spooned instant coffee into a china mug, filled the kettle, and was waiting for it to boil.

'You didn't have to clear away,' he said.

'We couldn't leave it for Mrs Green.'

'I would have done it later.'

Her eyes flashed in exasperation. 'Will you stop fussing, Oliver? It's done now.' She turned to the kettle and poured water over the coffee, added milk, stirred it, and then looked back at him.

Even those simplest actions fascinated him, made him realise what he was giving up. And all of a sudden he didn't know whether he could.

'I think I might take it up to my room,' said Anna.

'No, Anna, don't.' And without even stopping to think what message his actions would convey he reached out and took her into his arms.

# CHAPTER EIGHT

ANNA had the distinct feeling that if she didn't push Oliver away she was going to regret it.

He'd been on edge all evening, right from the moment he'd consoled her for dropping the stupid chicken. She hadn't been married to him for six months for nothing. She knew perfectly well how aroused he was, how much he wanted to make love to her.

The heat from him as they'd sat eating dinner had been tremendous. If they'd touched, he would have set her on fire. In fact, on the few occasions when his arm accidentally brushed hers, it had taken all her self-control not to move away. She'd almost expected to see her skin sear and shrivel.

'I think we should make ourselves comfortable in the sitting room,' he said, his voice a low warning growl that should have had her running for safety, but instead she allowed him to lead her from the kitchen.

Once in the other room, however, Anna quickly twisted away from him and dropped into one of the deep, plump armchairs. She saw from his frown that this wasn't exactly what he'd had in mind, but he said nothing, taking the matching, facing chair instead.

A fatal mistake, Anna realised at once. Oliver had always professed that he enjoyed watching her more than any other pastime. She too had once enjoyed being the object of his desire, had liked the feelings he aroused in her simply by looking at her. He could undress her with his eyes, make love to her with his eyes. It was a form of foreplay that she'd never experienced with anyone else, and doubted she ever would again.

Even now she could feel a stirring deep in her womb and deliberately she kept her eyes averted. But Oliver never took his eyes off her. Those wonderful tawny-gold eyes that had been her downfall in the very beginning.

Her coffee was growing cold but she didn't want to move for fear their eyes might meet and he would discover that she was as aroused as he, that she wanted to make love as much as he did. What a fateful night this was turning out to be.

'Drink your coffee.'

It was as though he had read her thoughts. She glanced across at him before she reached for it. Fatal. She couldn't drag her eyes away. They locked into his with all the force of a magnet on steel.

'Come here,' he whispered.

Anna swallowed and moistened her mouth, and her eyes darkened. 'What for?'

'As if you need to ask,' he growled.

The magnet pulled and Anna followed, her steps slow and resisting, but her eyes never leaving his. She was going to drown in them, she knew, and yet slavishly she went to her doom.

When she reached him he gave a groan and pulled her on to his lap. 'You're a witch, do you know that? An irresistible witch. You make me do things I hadn't planned to do; you make me break my own rules.'

Their mouths came together, a slow, sensual tasting

that lasted for ever. And then Oliver bade her kneel in front of him and he took the tab of her zip between his teeth and began to slowly draw it down.

It was one of the most erotic things he had ever done and Anna arched instinctively towards him, her breath coming in short, sharp gasps.

Oliver shuddered and his trembling fingers followed the line of the zip, stroking, appreciating, reacquainting, sending her female hormones into panic. And when he reached the bottom he finally lost patience.

He grabbed a handful of material in each hand and yanked it down over her shoulders, disposing of her bra with equally indecent haste, not content until her breasts were free of the restraining fabric, free for him to take into his palms, free for him to stroke his thumb deliciously over her erect and hungry nipples.

His teeth nipped and tortured, making her whimper with pleasure and ache for more. She held his head against her, loving the feel of his thick springy hair through her fingers.

It was wrong to let herself get carried away when there was no hope for the future, but wrong went out of the window when Oliver kissed her like this. It was almost as though he was worshipping her breasts.

He touched, he stroked; he licked, he sucked, and when he looked up at her there was a feverish light in his eyes. They were a more intense gold than she'd ever seen them, filled with such hot desire that it sent fresh shivers right through her.

'Oh, Oliver.' It was a cry she couldn't contain.

'Oh, Oliver, what?' he asked, still suckling.

'What you do to me.'

'What *I* do to you?' He lifted his head then. 'Have you any idea how I feel? You've worked your spell on me again, made me realise what I've been missing. This side of our marriage was never in dispute.'

Anna stiffened, their rare moment of togetherness in danger of being ruined—if it wasn't already. 'Are you saying that this is all you've ever wanted me for?' She sucked in her breath as she waited for his answer.

'It was an important part of it, Anna,' he admitted, his thumbs still stroking her now screamingly sensitised nipples. 'A very important part. I firmly believe that if the physical element goes out of a marriage it quickly disintegrates.'

Which told her precisely nothing. Theirs had disintegrated regardless of the fact that they still excited each other. It put his theory firmly out of the running, and suggested, even though he hadn't actually put it into words, that the delights of the flesh was all he'd ever wanted her for.

And she would be a fool to let it continue when he'd kick her out again as soon as she'd served her purpose. It made her wonder which purpose. Helping him sort his father's belongings? Or satisfying his carnal desires?

Surely he had Melanie for that? Or was it because he'd been with Melanie and she'd left him frustrated that he was doing this now? The thought was like a bitter pill too large to swallow and she shook her head. 'I can't go on with this, Oliver. You're right— sex is good between us, but it's not high on my list of priorities.'

Much!

'This is a mistake,' she added more quietly now as

she tried to back away from him. 'I don't know why I let myself get into this situation.'

Some of the light went out of his eyes. 'I thought it was because you wanted to?'

'I did, I do, but—it isn't right. We're on the verge of a divorce, Oliver. Have you forgotten that? How can we still make love?'

'I guess some things become a habit,' he admitted ruefully.

'Well, it's one habit you'll have to get out of,' she retorted, as she jumped to her feet and began tugging her suit back into place. Her bra was ignored. All she wanted to do was hide her pulsing breasts from his greedy eyes.

But it was the most awkward piece of clothing she owned and as she struggled to get her arms into the sleeves Oliver sprang up. 'Here, let me help.'

And begin the torture all over again!

'I can manage,' she said determinedly.

But it wasn't easy, especially as he stood and watched, especially when she saw the way his fingers clenched as she finally slid the zip back into place and there wasn't an inch of her body left for him to feast his eyes on. And yet she felt oddly sad that the evening which had promised such excitement had ended like this.

'I think I might go and catch up on some more work, after all,' he announced gruffly

Their eyes met and held and Anna saw sadness but she hardened her heart. She'd done the right thing. Emotional blackmail wasn't the answer. 'Don't do it on my account. I'm going to bed.'

But not to sleep, not for a long time. She'd had so

many sleepless nights since their marriage ended. So many nights when she'd lain awake thinking about Oliver and the good times they'd had. Could still have, if their experience earlier was anything to go by. But what good would it do? How would it help when at the end of the day he'd still divorce her?

The next morning Oliver was waiting for her at the breakfast table. He looked devastatingly casual in a pair of grey linen trousers, a blue shirt and a grey and blue cotton sweater—certainly not as though he was going to work up at the Hall.

Had he decided that their close proximity would be too much for him if she was going to insist that he keep his hands off her? Had he decided that putting distance between them was the only solution?

Anna didn't know whether to feel happy or sad. When she'd stopped him making love to her she hadn't wanted him to back off altogether, she'd simply wanted to cool things between them.

'I thought we'd have a change today,' he said cheerfully as she took her seat at the table.

Anna frowned, her heart spinning. So he wasn't rejecting her! 'What did you have in mind?'

'Maybe a trip on the river? Though it could be a tad cold. We could go into London, perhaps—shop, sightsee, take in a show?'

'I think you're forgetting I used to live in London,' she reminded him.

'As if I could forget anything about you.' His voice seemed to go down an octave as he spoke, his eyes warm as a summer day as they looked into hers.

Anna felt a tremor run through her. 'Actually, I am

homesick for the city. I think I'd like that.' There would be safety in crowds, unlike if they went river cruising when it would be just herself and Oliver. In London they'd be jostled and pushed and there'd be absolutely no chance of intimacy.

Even sorting Edward's stuff, there was always a forced togetherness which did nothing for her state of mind. A day away from it, a day doing something different, was exactly what she needed—what they both needed.

They caught the train and were in London by mid-morning and Anna thoroughly enjoyed strolling through the streets with Oliver. They explored the food hall in Harrods, ate lunch in style at Rules, one of London's oldest restaurants, and she tried on a blue and green chiffon evening dress which would be perfect around Christmas time. Although it was horrendously expensive Oliver persuaded her to buy it, and then settled the bill himself as she changed back into her street clothes.

'You shouldn't have done that,' she declared huffily. The expression on his face when he'd looked at her had frizzled her insides. It had suggested that he would get as much pleasure in stripping it off her as he would in seeing her in it.

Dark brows rose. 'I can't buy my wife clothes, is that what you're saying?'

'I'm no longer your wife,' she retorted.

His face shadowed but the next second he smiled with apparent unconcern. 'I can still buy you a present, can't I?'

Anna's pleasure was bittersweet. It wasn't quite the answer she would have liked.

They went to a show afterwards, an obscure musical that Anna didn't understand but which she pretended to enjoy, clapping energetically in all the right places and flashing Oliver approving glances.

All the big shows had been fully booked, this was the only one they'd been able to get tickets for, and over dinner afterwards Oliver said, 'You were very enthusiastic over that musical. I wasn't altogether sure it was your type.'

Anna wrinkled her nose. 'It wasn't. It wasn't yours either, was it?' They knew each too well to hide their true feelings.

'So has it spoilt your day?'

'Not at all,' she said immediately, fervently. 'I've thoroughly enjoyed myself. I feel guilty, though. You took time off work to organise things at the house and instead you're squiring me around.'

'Which I wouldn't have suggested if I hadn't wanted to do it. You're still a pleasure to be with.'

So why had he kicked her out of his life? Was this the moment to tell him about Chris, to explain exactly what she'd needed that thirty thousand pounds for? Would all be forgiven? Would she be satisfied with that? Or would she still feel disillusioned because he'd thought the worst of her in the first place?

'You're the sexiest woman in here, Anna, do you know that?' His voice had gone so low it sent shivers down her spine, her toes curling in her shoes 'I want you in my bed tonight. I can't live with you and not have you; it's driving me insane.'

Anna's hopes took a massive nosedive. He couldn't have made it any plainer what he wanted from her if he'd spelt it out in letters ten feet high. And once the house clearance was finished, it would be goodbye Anna.

Her eyes flashed a heated, brilliant green. 'If you can't handle my presence then perhaps I shouldn't stay. I'm not here for your convenience, Oliver; I thought I was helping with a particularly unpalatable job. If it's sex you're after, then ask Melanie—from what I can see, she'd be only too willing to oblige.'

He was clearly stunned by her reaction, his head jerking up, his eyes narrowed and questioning. 'You can't mean that, Anna?'

'Why can't I?'

'Because—because things are good between us.'

'You mean physically?' she asked sharply. 'If that's the only reason you accepted my offer, then I'll leave in the morning. You can finish off yourself or get Melanie to help.' She couldn't help throwing in the other woman's name again. 'She'd be delighted, I'm sure.'

'Let's leave Melanie out of this,' he growled.

'Why should we?' she shot back. 'I think she's very much a part of your life, despite what you say, and I don't think you need me.'

He closed his eyes for a moment as if trying to shut out her words. 'You really think that Melanie and I have got back together?'

Anna shrugged. 'It's how it looks.'

'Would it bother you if we had?'

It would hurt like hell, but she wasn't admitting it. 'Why should it when our marriage is over?' she asked instead. 'You're free to see whomever you like, do what you like with whomever you like. It has nothing to do with me any more. I think I'd like to go home,

Oliver.' She'd hardly touched her meal but it would choke her to try and eat now.

He didn't argue. He paid the bill and they left. They took a taxi to the station and neither of them spoke. But there was a half-hour wait for the train so they sat and drank coffee.

'Today was meant to be a happy occasion,' declared Oliver, swirling his drink vigorously in his cup. 'I wanted you to have a good time.'

'Which I have.'

'Until I spoiled it by admitting that your body drives me crazy,' he said with self-derision. 'Would it help if I apologised, Anna? If I said it was crass and insensitive of me to confess to such feelings— even if I felt them?'

Anna pulled a wry face and lifted her shoulders in a vague gesture. 'I'm flattered, but I don't understand. We're supposed to be separated. Why are you doing this to me?'

It was his turn to grimace. 'I guess there are some things that never go away.'

'Like sex, you mean?' she asked acidly. She tried to forget that it was all she'd thought about when she first met him. There had been an instant chemical flare of attraction, of desire, of goodness knew what, which they'd both mistaken for love.

Which was still there!

But it wasn't enough. A marriage needed more and she wasn't going to be sidetracked by that incredible passion again.

Oliver didn't answer her question. He looked pensively into his cup instead, holding it still now, and Anna guessed she had hit on the truth. She drank half of her coffee and then declared she needed to go to the loo. She didn't hurry and when she got back it was time for their train.

The journey was uncomfortably silent. There seemed nothing more to be said. It wasn't until they got home that Oliver asked whether she was still determined to leave.

'I'll stay and help until it's all done if you promise to behave,' she declared, looking him straight in the eye, making sure he knew she meant what she said. 'If you want me to, that is.'

Though why she was offering Anna had no idea. She had to be insane. It would be far safer to put as much distance between them as possible because, if the truth were known, she wanted his body as much as he wanted hers. And she had no doubt in her mind that it would always be that way.

'I'd like that.' Oliver nodded his agreement. 'But I can't—'

'Make any promises,' she finished for him. 'You don't have control over your male testosterone, is that what you're saying?'

'I guess I am.'

'So it will be up to me to keep you at arm's length? Very well, I can do that.' She spoke with confidence but her tingling nerves betrayed her real emotions. Keeping Oliver at bay would be like trying to ward off a hungry crocodile.

But, surprisingly, in the weeks that followed all went smoothly. Oliver never crossed the barriers she had rigidly imposed, though on several occasions she spotted him watching her hungrily.

His very real need of her caused her skin to burn

mercilessly, it sent a rash of scary emotions through her veins, and she had to busy herself elsewhere until the feelings went away.

Melanie came to see Oliver several times but on each occasion he told her that he was too busy to take her out, and that he didn't need any further help. Anna wondered how hard it was for him to deny his body what it craved.

If it was pure sex that drove him, surely Melanie could fulfil those needs? Or had she misjudged him? Did he want to give their marriage another go? Was that behind everything? And, if so, why hadn't he said? Why didn't he tell her what he was thinking, feeling, expecting?

Instead, most days he worked in silence, talking only of the work in hand, sometimes saying he'd never realised what a large task it was.

'You're forgetting that Edward's lifetime is here,' she said as Oliver sorted through file after file in his father's cabinets, while she kept busy packing the hundreds of books which Oliver wanted to keep.

'Are you telling me his whole life is being packed into carboard boxes? That this is the way we all end?'

'I guess it's something like that,' she agreed. 'It's sad, isn't it?'

'And I've had enough for today.' He lifted his arms above his head and stretched and Anna had an imbecilic urge to go to him, to press her hungry body close to his. This constant togetherness was telling on her, making her wonder whether she'd made the right decision.

And if it was telling on her, what was it doing to Oliver? She'd heard him prowling his room at night and once she'd heard him come to her door. He had stood there for a long time before he'd quietly gone back.

She'd become very tense, holding her breath, straining her ears, and wishing, much to her disgust, that he'd give up on his promise and come and make fantasic love to her.

Of course, if he had come in, she'd probably have ordered him straight out again—but the things it did to her simply thinking about it were enough to spin her mind into orbit.

But at least they never fell out. He was politeness itself, always courteous, always thoughtful, almost too much so. Sometimes she could have screamed at the correctness of his behaviour.

Then one day the perfect veneer crashed. She was on her knees on the upstairs landing carefully sorting sheets and pillowcases into sets when he came storming towards her, eyes like twin flames of fire. 'I should have known I couldn't trust you.'

Anna looked up at Oliver in frank amazement. 'What are you talking about? What am I supposed to have done now?' And she knew by the look on his face that it had to be something dire.

# CHAPTER NINE

'I'M TALKING about family heirlooms.' Oliver didn't take his eyes off Anna's face for one single second. 'Diamonds and sapphires that belonged to my grandmother. My great-grandfather's gold hunter watch.'

'And what have they to do with me?' she asked indignantly, feeling an unhealthy chill steal down her spine.

'Do you dare to ask?' he thrust, his face red with rage, 'when you're the only person who's been left alone in this house since my father died?'

Anna went very still and very cold. 'You're suggesting I took them?'

'Who else?'

'Perhaps you'd like to search my room?' She found it hard to believe that Oliver was accusing her of theft. One minute he'd wanted to take her to bed; now he looked as though he'd like to strangle her with his bare hands.

Perhaps it was as well their marriage had ended.

This was a side of him she'd never seen before, at least not to this degree. He'd been angry about the money, but this time he was so enraged he was dancing on the balls of his feet and his golden eyes leapt with fire.

'As if that would turn up anything,' he tossed scornfully. 'We both know what's happened to the stuff, don't we? That little story about seeing your brother again was nothing more than a cover-up. Well, let me tell you, lady, this time you've gone too far. You had a legitimate excuse where the money was concerned, but not now.'

Anna tried her hardest to keep her dignity because she knew that yelling back at him would get her nowhere. But it was difficult when confronted by such a fierce and unrelenting condemnation.

'Oliver—'

'Don't!'

'Don't what?' she asked with a quick frown, wishing she hadn't felt the usual rush of adrenalin. She didn't need anything that would let her down.

'Don't try to get out of it.'

'You're jumping to conclusions.'

'I wish I was.'

'I haven't been anywhere near your father's precious jewellery. I didn't even know it existed.'.

'And I'm supposed to believe that, am I?'

'It's the truth.'

'So where the hell is it?'

'I don't know. If you don't want to believe me, that's your prerogative, but I've not seen it, I've not taken it, and I've not given it to Tony.'

For a fraction of a second he looked as though he wanted to believe her, but then his face hardened again, the rage continued. 'Tony's address—please.'

The 'please' was an afterthought, but he could have dropped to his knees and begged and it would have got him nowhere because she had no idea where Tony was. There had been no contact between them since he'd called off their engagement.

'I don't have it.'

'Liar!' he ground through his teeth.

Anger welled in Anna like a pan of milk on the boil. 'I have never lied to you, Oliver, and I'm not lying now. I don't know where your damn jewellery is. Maybe your father got rid of it. Have you seen it since he died? Where did he keep it?'

'In the safe—and yes, I've seen it.'

'So how was I—' Anna touched her two hands to her chest '—supposed to have taken it?'

'Because the key to the safe was with the rest of the house keys. It was labelled ''cellar,'' apparently to confuse any potential burglar—but you had plenty of time to try all the keys before you took off in the Land Rover.'

'Are you sure it doesn't have a combination lock as well, which I'm miraculously supposed to have known?' she asked scathingly. 'This is ridiculous, Oliver. I'm not going to listen to any more of your accusations.'

Anna was so incensed she could have hit him. Had their relationship disintegrated to such a degree that Oliver thought her capable of stealing? She swept savagely past him, shaking off his arm as he tried to stop her, running quickly down the stairs, and storming out of the house.

At the Lodge she phoned for a taxi. Then she ran up to her room, snatched her case from the top of the wardrobe and flung her clothes into it. By the time she had finished, when every last possession was packed, the taxi had arrived.

Anna was still spitting fire as she left behind the house where she had once been so happy. The sad part was, Oliver hadn't even come after her.

She had a long wait at the airport. Turning up without a ticket or with any thought as to what time the next plane to Dublin was hadn't been a very good move. What it did do was give her time to think.

And at the end of all her thinking she knew that she was doing the right thing. Trying to mend bridges never worked. Twice Oliver had hurt her; he was not going to get the chance to do it again.

She was extremely bitter and deeply hurt that he'd thought her capable of stealing his family heirlooms. It proved that he'd never really loved her. Sex had, as she'd suspected, been the only common bond between them.

If he had loved her, he'd have trusted her implicitly; he wouldn't have thought for even one second that she was responsible. She was well rid of him.

It was late evening and dark when Anna arrived at the cottage. She was cold and tired and considerably out of sorts. She switched on the electric fire in the living room, filled the kettle and put that on to boil, then went upstairs and switched on the electric blanket.

That done, she emptied her suitcase unceremoniously on to the spare bed, telling herself that she would put everything away in the morning. She sorted out a nightdress and dressing gown and undressed in front of the fire downstairs. She made herself a mug of drinking chocolate, ate half a packet of biscuits, because she was suddenly starving, and then went to bed.

And amazingly she slept for ten hours. When she opened her eyes she couldn't remember where she was, but it didn't take long for the whole sorry affair to come flooding back.

Was Oliver glad to be rid of her, she wondered sadly, or would he come chasing after her demanding to know what she'd done with the jewellery? He'd be in for a big disappointment if he did, because she hadn't a clue what had happened to it.

What she did know was that her marriage to Oliver was definitely over; it was a part of her life best forgotten, a closed chapter. Today she was going to make a fresh start.

She jumped out of bed, showered and dressed, plucked a loaf out of the freezer, toasted a couple of slices, made a big pot of coffee, and spent the next hour thinking about her future.

For the time being, she'd stay here. She'd get a temporary job again in Wexford, and once she felt up to it she would return to London and settle back into her old life.

She'd made a big mistake in marrying Oliver, the biggest mistake of her life. Love at first sight, marrying on an impulse, rarely worked. She should have known that; she'd heard it said enough times.

Anna spent the day settling in, shopping for food, and generally making herself comfortable. Tomorrow she planned to go job-hunting.

Oliver couldn't believe he had accused Anna of stealing. The Anna he had married would never do something like that. Not in a million years. The money that she'd taken was a different matter altogether—she'd seen that as her own and he shouldn't have judged her now on the strength of what she'd done then.

But what was he to believe? Where had the jewellery gone? Who had taken it? Looking at the situation logically, Anna was the only one who'd had the keys to the Hall, who'd had the opportunity.

He'd seen the gems in the safe in the days after the funeral—and now they were gone—and Anna had paid a visit to her mysterious brother again! Everything pointed to her—and yet deep down inside him he knew that she wasn't guilty. He should never have accused her; he was the world's biggest idiot.

The trouble was she'd been driving him insane for weeks with her tempting body and her enticing green eyes. Every time she looked at him he'd felt a surge of hunger, a very real need to take her to bed again and make wild passionate love.

It kept him awake at night and tormented him during the day and the time had been drawing close when he could hang on to his emotions no longer. It was why he had snapped. Why he had accused her. Why he hadn't been thinking straight.

And now it was too late.

Oliver had wanted to stop Anna on that fateful day; he'd wanted to go after her, tell her he'd been mistaken, that he'd made his accusation in the heat of the moment and he knew he was wrong. But he also knew that he needed to give her time to calm down.

So he'd waited a couple of hours before returning to the Lodge—then had the shock of his life when he discovered that she'd disappeared and taken everything with her.

He had thought she meant that she wasn't staying at the Hall, not that she was leaving him altogether. Damn! What was he to do now? Was there any chance for them or had he well and truly ruined any future prospects?

Accusing Anna had been a moment of madness. His blind fury had killed her love for him. Killed it stone dead.

He poured a whisky and tossed it down his throat. In fact, he had several whiskies and he spent the rest of the day in a self-induced alcoholic haze, trying to convince himself that he was better off without Anna.

In the cold light of dawn, he knew differently. His head throbbed, his mouth felt like a sewer, but he knew that he had to find her. He loved her too much to let her go without a fight. She was sure to have gone to the cottage to pick up her car. With a bit of luck, she'd stay a few days and he would find her there.

When Melanie phoned just as he was about to ring up and book his flight, he cut her short. He didn't want Melanie hanging around any more. He'd done his duty; he'd been nice to her while she was grieving over Edward, but enough was enough.

And when it rang again immediately afterwards he barked fiercely, 'Melanie, I thought I'd told you—'

'I don't know who Melanie is but it's definitely not me.'

Oliver was momentarily taken aback by the man's amused voice. 'I'm sorry, who is this?'

'Chris Paige, Anna's brother. Is she there?'

Anna's brother! The mysterious brother whom he'd never been allowed to meet.

'No, she isn't,' he said perhaps more sharply than he intended, but he could do without these calls at this precise moment.

'When will she be home? I really would like to speak to her.'

Oliver closed his eyes and leant his head back against the chair. 'Never.' Had he really said that, or was it only in his mind?

'What do you mean never?'

Oh, Lord, he had said it. He'd have to tell the truth now. 'She's left me.'

There was a short, palpable silence before Chris said slowly, 'Because of the money she lent me? Were you still hassling her over that?'

So it was her brother after all that Anna had given the money to, and she'd told Chris about his reaction. What sort of a fiend did that make him? And while Oliver was still wondering how to answer, Chris spoke again.

'Did she ever tell you the real reason she lent it to me?'

'No,' Oliver admitted quietly, rubbing a hand over his throbbing brow.

'It was because I made her promise not to,' admitted Chris. 'I did eventually release her from that promise but it was my fault all the same that you never got to hear the truth.'

'A promise?' What was the man talking about?

'I needed money; my business was in trouble. I knew it was only a temporary thing, but—'

'And you made Anna promise not to tell me?' cut in Oliver impatiently. 'For goodness' sake, I'd have lent you the money myself if I'd known, if Anna had spoken up.' None of this made any sense.

But when Chris finished explaining, Oliver had to admit that Langford Properties probably wouldn't have put the business his way if they'd known he was in financial trouble.

'So what are you going to do about my sister?' asked Chris, swiftly dismissive of talk about work.

'I'm going after her,' Oliver declared firmly. 'Though whether she'll have me back is another story. I've said some distinctly terrible things to her.'

'I guess you have plenty of humble pie to eat. Anna has lots of pride, you know. But, for what it's worth, I think she still loves you. Good luck.'

As Oliver put down the phone he knew he would need all the luck he could get. Chris didn't know the whole story. He'd probably never have suggested attempting a reconciliation if he did. He would have told Oliver to keep well away from his sister with his ridiculous and unfounded accusations.

# CHAPTER TEN

ANNA had been expecting Oliver ever since Chris's phone call; she'd even stood at the window most of the day watching and waiting. At first she'd thought about scooting off somewhere, to London maybe, somewhere where he wouldn't find her.

But she'd decided ultimately that the confrontation had to be made, final decisions reached. Divorce was her only option. There was no point in remaining married to a man who didn't trust her, who would never trust her.

Chris had tried to persuade her to give it another go, but Anna knew that she daren't, couldn't, wouldn't. 'He's not getting the chance to hurt me again,' she'd declared fiercely.

She gave up her vigil when it grew dark. He wasn't coming. Not today, anyway. Thank goodness. All this nervous agitation for nothing. She was in the kitchen preparing a light supper when Oliver pounded on the door. The sudden sound frightened her but she knew instinctively that it was him.

Her legs felt as though they were filled with lead as she made her way to the front door. It took an age for her to get there. And when she opened it she didn't stand back for Oliver to enter but waited for him to speak, snapping on the outside light so that she could see him more clearly.

He looked dreadful. His golden eyes were sunk into

deeply shadowed sockets, his cheeks were drawn, and it pleased her that he'd been suffering, too. Why should she be the only one to feel like hell?

'Anna.' He nodded.

So he wasn't going to make the opening move; he was leaving it up to her. 'Hello, Oliver. I've been expecting you.' She deliberately kept her voice icy cold and impersonal. 'A pity you didn't phone, first. It would have saved you a journey.'

'I understand that I'm not welcome,' he said, his eyes narrowing on her pale face. 'But surely you're not going to turn me away?'

'Is there any reason why I shouldn't?' she asked sharply. 'Didn't I make it clear that it's all over between us?'

'We need to talk,' he said.

'Why?' she asked heatedly. 'Because you've found out about the promise I made Chris? That I really do have a brother? It makes a difference, does it?' She was ready to spit fire. If he thought he could come here and apologise and it would make things all right again then he was deeply mistaken.

'It doesn't make a difference—of course not,' he retorted. 'I was in the wrong and I admit that. Now can I please come in?'

Anna could see that she was not going to get away with keeping him on the doorstep so she reluctantly stepped aside, though she heaved a sigh to show her disapproval. 'You've wasted your time. Nothing you can say will make any difference to how I feel.'

No man truly in love with his wife would accuse her of stealing family jewellery, he would at least discuss it first. But not Oliver. Oh, no, he'd acted first and thought last. And now, having realised that he'd made a mistake, it looked as though he wanted to put matters right.

And pigs might fly!

Anna closed the door behind Oliver and followed him through to the sitting room. It was a tiny room, nothing at all like the handsomely proportioned sitting room at Weston Lodge. And there was no escaping him.

His devastating masculinity filled the cramped space; his cologne invaded it; his very presence was a threat to her sanity. 'Now say what you've got to say and then go,' she said crisply, trying not to look at him, but it was impossible.

Oliver Langford could not be ignored. He wore the same black squidgy leather jacket that he had on the fateful day they'd first met, black sweater, black jeans. Sexy, dismayingly exciting.

He stood, apparently waiting for her to be seated before he took a chair himself. And Anna, who had been determined to remain standing, who had no intention of encouraging him to linger, found her legs would hold her up no longer. Please don't let him stay long, she prayed, as she slid down on to the nearest chair. I'm not up to this.

Oliver sat too. 'I made a huge mistake.'

'I won't argue with that,' she said. 'Is that why you're here, to apologise?'

'Something like that.' And then he frowned. 'Are you all right, Anna? You look very pale. Are you eating properly?'

Oh, Lord, she hoped he wasn't going to question her over her health. There were some things she'd rather he didn't know. 'Of course I'm eating,' she snapped. 'As a matter of fact, I was just making myself some supper.'

'Then make it supper for two. I'm famished.'

Anna groaned. Did he have to add to her torment? 'It's only a tuna sandwich.'

'I like tuna.'

'And some salad.'

'That's good.' He pushed himself up. 'I'll come and help, shall I?'

Help or hinder? She needed neither. 'There's not really room for two in the kitchen, as you very well know. I can manage on my own. You stay here. I'll bring it in on a tray.'

'I seem to remember we worked well together at one time,' he said with a sudden gleam in his eye. 'It was a very cosy arrangement.'

Yes, so cosy that their bodies continually brushed against each other. It had been an exercise in physical excitement. They'd even made love in the kitchen. But that was then and this was now, and she didn't want any reminders.

'Cosy arrangements are no longer the order of the day,' she told him coolly. 'You'd best remember that. I'd rather you stay here.'

He shrugged. 'You're the boss.' And reluctantly he sat down again.

When Anna reached the kitchen she stood with her back to the wall and took in several deep, steadying breaths. Although she'd been expecting Oliver, had decided exactly what she was going to say to him, she hadn't been prepared for this adrenalin rush.

She had thought that every single one of her feelings had been destroyed, she'd thought all that remained was hatred. How, then, could she explain the fact that her insides had sizzled simply by looking at him?

Or was she receiving mixed signals? Was it sizzling hatred and not desire? Was it resentment that pulsed through her veins not hunger? How could she be sure? She did know, though, that if she didn't hurry and finish the sandwiches he would come in search of her.

The thought electrified her into action and ten minutes later all was ready. Oliver had thoughtfully moved the coffee table between the two chairs and she set down the tray, congratulating herself on appearing calm and untroubled when it was a far cry from the feelings churning inside her.

They spoke little over supper although Anna knew it wouldn't be long before Oliver started on what he'd really come here for. Was it to apologise? Was it to beg her forgiveness? Was it to say he'd made a grave error of judgement? Or was it to sort out their divorce?

'What are you thinking?'

Anna looked across at Oliver. He had stopped eating and was watching her intently with those devastating golden eyes.

'You were very deep in thought,' he said. 'Troubled thought. Did it concern me?'

'Naturally.' It would have been stupid to claim otherwise.

'We have a lot of talking to do,' he admitted.

'Yes.'

'It was wrong of me to accuse you of taking those heirlooms.'

'I'm glad you realise it.'

'I should have known you'd never do a thing like that.'

'Yes, you should have.'

'I should also have known that you had a very good reason for using that thirty thousands pounds.' His lips twisted wryly. 'I shouldn't have tarred you with the same brush as Rosemary and Melanie.'

'And do you feel better now you've said all that?' she asked tartly.

Oliver's hands gripped the arms of his chair until his knuckles gleamed white. He clearly hadn't expected quite so much antagonism. But his voice remained calm. 'I'm asking your forgiveness.'

'No you're not.' Anna shook her head firmly. 'You're trying to make amends. But it won't work. You've hurt me far too much. You could get down on your knees and it would make no difference.'

'Anna—'

'Anna, nothing,' she shot. 'We're finished; it's over. I doubt we ever really loved each other. If we had there wouldn't have been these problems, you'd have trusted me, you'd have let me explain. We enjoyed good sex but that was all. Your father was right to oppose the marriage. He was the only one with any sense.'

Oliver rubbed his fingers over his brow. 'You've changed, Anna. You were never this hard before. You always—'

'Is it any wonder I've changed,' she cut in, widening her eyes and looking at him scornfully, 'after the way you treated me? I don't want you in my life any more, Oliver. If you've come here to grovel and beg me to go back with you, then forget it, because I won't. I'd actually prefer it if you left.' Please, God, she was doing the right thing.

'At this time of night?'

'Yes, at this time of night. It's your fault for coming so late.'

'I couldn't get an earlier flight.'

'Then you should have waited until tomorrow.'

'I was hoping you'd let me stay?'

Anna groaned. This was the last thing she wanted. 'I don't think so.'

'Not even if I promise not to hassle you? If I promise to be a good boy?'

He pulled such a forlorn face and it was such a ridiculous thing for him to say that Anna's good intentions went flying out the window. 'Provided you leave at first light,' she reluctantly agreed. 'I don't want you here, Oliver. It's over between us and the sooner you accept it, the better.'

He winced at her harsh words. 'There must be some way I can get you to change your mind?'

'None at all,' she retorted. 'If you want to go to bed now, you know where the spare room is. I'll clear away here.'

'No, please, let me help.' He sprang to his feet and picked up the tray.

'In that case, you can do it all. I'll go to bed,' she said tightly. 'Goodnight, Oliver.' He didn't look pleased but she didn't care, and she was safely tucked up under the covers when she heard him mount the stairs.

She had brushed her teeth and washed her face in record time so that she wouldn't bump into him again. But she wasn't able to relax and she found herself listening and waiting.

Her fingers curled and her whole body stiffened when he reached her bedroom door, even her heart thudded, but he passed on by without a falter in his step. He went into the bathroom, which separated the two rooms, she heard water running and the toilet flushing, and then she heard him go into the spare room. After that there was silence but still she didn't relax.

She imagined him undressing. Stripping off his sweater and jeans, his shoes and socks, the brief plain underpants he always wore. And as he hadn't brought an overnight bag she imagined him sleeping nude between the clean cotton sheets. The very thought of his magnificent firm body was more than enough to send her into spasm.

It was a long time before she slept.

The next morning she hoped and prayed that Oliver would have taken her at her word and gone before she ventured downstairs, but she had no such luck. He even had breakfast ready. But the smell of crispy bacon as she walked into the kitchen was more than Anna's stomach could stand.

She rushed back up to the bathroom, desperately hoping Oliver hadn't heard her. When she finally rejoined him breakfast had been cleared away. There was a coffee pot on the go but that was all. He looked at her in concern. 'I know there's something wrong with you, Anna. Why don't you tell me what it is?'

'I must have picked up a bug,' she said airily. 'I think I'll have some toast.' She needed action, anything so that she wouldn't have to look at Oliver. Whether she would eat the toast was a different matter altogether.

'I'm expected to believe that, am I?' he asked shortly. 'You've seen a doctor? He's told you it's a bug?'

'Not yet, I haven't,' she answered with a shrug. 'It's only just come on. Don't worry about it, Oliver, I'll be all right.'

But she could feel his eyes boring into her back as she popped bread into the toaster. And while she was waiting she filled the kettle. 'I think I'd like tea rather than coffee. Do you want a cup?'

'No, thank you, Anna.' Such polite words.

She would have liked to turn around and look at him but knew that she daren't. Her heart pumped uneasily. Then she told herself that she was being silly because how could he possibly have guessed? When her toast was made and the tea poured Oliver took it from her and carried it through to the sitting room. In those idyllic days when they first met, they'd always eaten at the window table where they could watch the birds in the garden, the freshness of spring, the weather over the Wicklow Mountains. So there was nothing unusual in him carrying her breakfast there.

And yet Anna still had this peculiar feeling. It was probably guilt, she decided, as she sat down and picked up a piece of toast. Guilt because she'd made a conscious decision to hide her condition from him.

She nibbled a corner and kept her eyes averted.

Oliver sat the other side of the table, the pot of coffee in front of him.

'I think it's more than just a bug,' he said quietly. 'Don't you think you ought to tell me?'

Anna frowned and felt her stomach begin to churn again, though for a very different reason this time. 'I don't know what you're talking about.'

'Oh, I think you do. Look at me, Anna. Tell me truthfully what is wrong.'

'There is nothing wrong,' she insisted, but she still couldn't bring herself to look at him.

'I looked in your bathroom cabinet this morning for a spare toothbrush.'

Alarm bells rang. Big alarm bells.

'And guess what I saw, Anna?'

She remained silent.

'A pregnancy testing kit.'

She wanted to slide beneath the table, she wanted to disappear into a hole in the ground. She could brazen it out and say, So what? She could say that she'd used it and it had proved negative. She could say lots of things—but at the end of the day he would find out.

Oliver wasn't stupid. He could see the state she was in. Her morning sickness had come on early and there was no way she could hide it.

If only she hadn't stopped taking the Pill that first time she left him. She'd been experiencing problems and intended trying a different one. Meanwhile, she had decided to give her body a rest.

Stupidly, she hadn't given it a thought when she let Oliver make love to her. They'd both been fired with the passion of the moment and contraception had been the last thing on their minds.

A fatal mistake. One of many she had made where this man was concerned.

She eyed him bravely. 'And do you know what, Oliver? It tested positive. Not that it's going to make very much difference to you, because this baby's mine.'

It was a decision she'd made when she first discovered that she was pregnant. She didn't want him as the father. He had well and truly given up that right. 'I'm not coming back to you. I'll naturally let you—'

'The hell you aren't coming back!' It was a mighty roar and almost lifted the rafters. Then Oliver must have realised that this was no way to get what he wanted because his voice went much quieter.

'This baby is mine as much as yours, Anna. I presume it is mine?' He said it as an afterthought, not really believing that it was anyone else's.

'Of course.'

'Therefore I want to be a part of it, I want to be there for you, help you through this bad time. You must see a doctor. It will be best if you come home with me and see the family doctor. I'll make the arrangements, I'll—'

'Oliver.' Anna's tone was firm. 'I'm not coming back to a man who thinks I stole the family jewels.'

She was pleased to note that he had the grace to look ashamed. As well he should.

'I'm not giving you any choice, Anna,' he said, fingers strumming on the table. 'The truth is that I accused you without thinking. I realised immediately that you would never have done such a thing. You're too honest, too straight, too good.'

He added these last two words with a wry twist of his lips. 'Too good for me. I know I can never repair the damage I've inflicted, but for the sake of our baby—' he smiled as he said the words '—I'm begging you to give me one last chance. I promise I will never, ever, accuse you of stealing again. Or of marrying me for money.'

'You're right—you won't, because you won't get the chance,' she told him surely. It was no good him making promises because if he'd done it twice what was to say he wouldn't do it a third time? She refused to take the risk.

He frowned harshly. 'You really mean that you won't come home with me, Anna.'

'Yes.' She had thought it through very carefully and decided it was the right thing to do. 'I'll let you have access, I shan't be petty enough to deny you that, but—'

'For God's sake, woman, what do I have to do? Get down on my knees and beg?'

'That I would like to see,' she tossed the words at him bitterly, 'but it still wouldn't be enough. Nothing will. I don't think you have any idea how much you've hurt me. I shall never forgive you, not as long as I live. So I can't see the point in us living together. It would put us both into an impossible situation.'

# CHAPTER ELEVEN

OLIVER couldn't even begin to describe his feelings when he'd seen that pregnancy testing kit. Shock at first, complete and utter shock. He'd stared at it for several minutes, his heart banging against his ribs, before deciding it was a relic left behind by Anna's sister.

But maybe not.

Maybe it was Anna's!

Alarm set in then—but only because their marriage wasn't working. The thought of Anna having a baby, his baby, brought a rush of paternal warmth, a joy he had never experienced before.

And he'd known as soon as he'd seen how ill Anna looked when she came downstairs that she was pregnant. She'd been pale the night before but he'd put that down to exhaustion. This was something different.

He'd quietly followed her up to the bathroom and heard her retching, and so he'd returned to the kitchen and got rid of everything that could induce nausea.

He knew when it had happened but he didn't know how when she was on the Pill. But if anything could mend their marriage, bring them back together, it was surely this. He had been unprepared, therefore, when she'd flatly refused to go home with him.

An impossible situation she had said and he could see how her mind worked. What he needed to do was somehow, some way, persuade her to return with him. And once he'd got her home he could work on her. Convince her that he would never let her down again, that it was the worst mistake he'd ever made in his life, and that this was the best thing that could have happened to them.

It might be a long haul but he loved Anna so desperately that he was prepared to do anything to save their marriage.

'You can't stay here alone, Anna,' he said quietly. 'Not in your condition.'

'I shan't feel sick for ever so why shouldn't I?' she snapped, her emerald eyes glaring magnificently.

She was so beautiful, so desirable, that he couldn't imagine why he had endangered their marriage by accusing her of crimes that he knew she wasn't capable of committing. He could only plead insanity due to sexual frustration.

'I want you home because you're my wife,' he said patiently. 'I want to look after you, take care of you, make things easier for you.'

Her eyes flashed again. 'Belated concern, Oliver? Are you forgetting that you're the one who made things hard for me?'

She couldn't have hurt him any more if she'd struck him with an axe. 'You think I don't know that? You think it won't haunt me for the rest of my life?'

He was aware that the pain he felt filled his voice. He wanted her to hear it, he wanted her to know that he truly regretted what he had done. 'Anna, I want to make it up to you. You must give me that chance.'

He saw the way she looked at him, the flash of indignance, followed by uncertainty as their eyes briefly met, the way she averted them again quickly as though she was afraid of giving something away. Hope flooded through him. It looked as though she wasn't as immune to him as she was trying to make out.

There had always been a strong chemical attraction, a raging fire that had drawn them irresistibly together and in that one tiny instant he had seen it again. Admittedly, a faint spark only. But in that spark there was hope. Her fire wasn't dead—he hadn't killed it— and if it was the last thing he did he would nurture it back to precious life.

He pressed home his minuscule advantage. 'Anna, you have my word that I will never hurt you again. This is our child you are carrying, conceived through an act of love.' Hopefully she wouldn't negate that. 'Will your conscience let you deny your child its father?'

He wanted to go on and say it would want for nothing but that would mean bringing the money issue into it again—and this was something he needed to avoid like the plague. It would be like holding a red rag to a bull. She would turn on him again and all hope would be lost.

'My conscience has nothing to do with it, Oliver,' she told him coldly. 'You're the one who's made me feel this way. You can't go around flinging accusations and then expect to welcome me back into your arms the next minute as though nothing has happened.'

'I know that,' he admitted ruefully. 'Don't you think I've paid the penalty? But we're not talking about you, now, we're talking about the child. It's not only me who needs you—it's our baby, too.'

They had spoken of having a family many times, though they hadn't planned it quite this soon. And they had agreed that a child needed both parents—they had said that if ever the unthinkable happened and their marriage foundered they would stick together for the sake of any children they might have. Had she forgotten that?'

Anna took a long, deep breath, closed her eyes and for several long, never-ending seconds, appeared to consider his words. Faint hope rose in him, but when she spoke it wasn't what he wanted to hear. 'I'm sorry, Oliver, it wouldn't work.'

'We could make it work,' he said softly. 'I cannot envisage life without you. I'm not using our baby as blackmail—well, maybe just a little,' he added with a self-deprecating grimace. 'But I need you, too. You mean the whole world to me. These last two days have been the blackest of my life.'

'Oliver,' she said with a touch of impatience, 'I've already given this a lot of thought. I don't see how I can live with a man who distrusts me. It wouldn't work. I'd be forever waiting for the next time.'

'There won't be a next time,' he promised her firmly. It hurt deep in his gut that she should even think this. Hadn't his apologies been enough? Hadn't she believed him? What more could he say?

Anna shook her head. 'It's easy for you to say that, Oliver. I've discovered a side to you that I hadn't known existed, and one that I don't like. Have you really no idea how I feel? I have never stolen so much as a penny in my life. You have hurt and humiliated me, you made me feel like the lowest of the low, and yet you now expect me to come back and live with you, put myself up for more of the same, just because I'm carrying your baby. It's not on, Oliver. I can't do it.'

His faint spark of hope died. Short of using cave-man tactics and physically carrying her back home, what was he to do? He had never seen Anna so determined. And so magnificently beautiful in her anger.

He wanted to bed her there and then, make exciting, uninhibited love like they had in the early days of their marriage. Would that work? Would she agree to anything once they were locked in each other's arms, unable to get enough of each other?

But he knew that emotional blackmail wasn't the answer. Anna had to come back because she wanted to, because she knew it would be best for her and the baby.

He poured himself another cup of coffee while he decided what to say next, noticing as he did so that Anna hadn't touched her toast; there was still only one tiny bite gone from the corner. She hadn't touched her tea, either.

'How can I prove that I won't accuse you of anything like that ever again, if you don't give me the chance?' He was prepared to go down on his knees and beg if he thought it would help. He'd never been in a situation like this before. Most things he could talk his way around, but with Anna so stubborn...

'Maybe you should have thought of that before you made your allegations.'

Oliver groaned. 'As if I haven't done that a thousand times already. Anna—' he leant forward urgently and took her hands across the table '—I don't want you to go through this alone. I want to be there at your side. You need me. You can't tell me that you're looking forward to being alone during what should be one of the most exciting and rewarding times of your life?'

She closed her eyes, shut him out, didn't let him see whatever she was thinking. But he was almost sure he had got through to her. At least she didn't snatch her hands away.

'What would happen if you became ill while you were living alone?' he urged. 'Even now, with this morning sickness, you need someone with you. Anna, please come back with me—even if it's only until the baby's born. At least give yourself a chance, give me a chance to prove that I do truly love you and I'll never hurt you again.'

Her eyes slowly opened and in their green depths he thought he saw hesitation, uncertainty.

'If,' he went on, 'once the baby's born, you decide that you cannot bear to live with me a moment longer, then I will let you go.' Though he hoped it never came to that. He hoped time would prove to her that he meant what he said, because how could he let go the woman he loved more than life itself?

He would do whatever it took. He would demonstrate in every way possible that his love was unswerving and loyal, that he trusted her implicitly in all things.

'*If* I come,' she said eventually, 'and it's a very big if, it will be under one condition.'

The words were music to his ears. 'Name it,' he

said magnanimously. Nothing could be worse than her not coming at all.

'That we continue to sleep in separate rooms,' she said firmly, her eyes almost glaring now, expecting him to object. 'It will be a marriage in name only for the sake of the baby.'

It was not the answer he wanted but it was better than nothing. It hurt like hell that she didn't want to sleep with him, but hopefully she would change her mind once she realised how deep his feelings for her were, once she accepted that he would never hurt her again. It was a matter, he supposed, of earning her trust.

He nodded slowly. 'If that's what you really want.'

'It is,' she declared firmly.


Anna knew that she had to be out of her mind agreeing to Oliver's request, but the truth was she didn't relish the idea of going through this pregnancy on her own. Oliver had hit on the truth—she was afraid of it. Perhaps all new mothers-to-be felt this way? She didn't know.

And although all trust between them had been destroyed she did still, surprisingly, love Oliver. Why, she didn't know considering the way he had treated her, but she did. Not that she was going to let him see it. Although how hard that would be was anyone's guess.

They couldn't get a ferry until the following day and it was late evening by the time they got home. Anna hated to admit it but it really did feel like home when she walked into Weston Lodge.

They had, after all, spent six happy months here

and it had the familiar feel of a place where love had reigned supreme. It was such a pity that Oliver had ruined everything.

Oliver put her bags into the room she had used when she was here last. 'This is what you want?' he asked with grave concern. 'You don't have to sleep in here, you know. I'd much rather you—'

'It's what I want,' she declared firmly.

'Can I help you unpack?'

'No, thanks.' Another brisk retort. 'I can manage on my own.'

'Then I'll ask Mrs G to make us a drink and perhaps a sandwich.'

Anna shook her head. 'Don't bother on my part. I'm tired. I'm going straight to bed.'

Oliver frowned. 'You are all right, Anna? It's been a long day, I know. Are you sure that—?'

'Oliver, I am very sure.' Her eyes flashed her irritation. 'All I want to do is sleep.' Last night had been stressful; she'd hardly slept a wink. All the time she'd kept thinking that Oliver might come waltzing into her room. And the truth was, she wouldn't have been able to keep him at bay. No matter what her head told her, her heart dictated otherwise. And she guessed it always would.

Oliver too had been unable to sleep. She'd heard him go downstairs just after two and had been sorely tempted to follow, hoping that a hot drink might settle her. But it had been too big a risk to take.

Her feelings ran far too high for such close contact. She would have ended up in his arms—and what good would that have done? He would have thought she'd forgiven him and she hadn't. It was doubtful she ever would.

But would she be able to sleep tonight, despite how tired she was? Would she still worry that he might come to her, that her body would give way to its cravings? They were questions she couldn't answer.

'I'll say goodnight, then, Anna.' Oliver gave her a chaste kiss on the brow. 'If there is anything you need just—'

'Please go, Oliver. I'm all right; I'm only tired. Stop fussing.'

He went then, reluctantly, and Anna flung herself down on the bed fully clothed. Had she made a mistake in allowing him to persuade her to come back here? Was he going to watch over her like a mother hen? Smother her?

She closed her eyes. She didn't want that. She wanted to be left alone; she wanted to do things her way without him interfering or fussing. He had lost all right to be a husband to her. Tomorrow she would make that very plain.

Anna fell into an immediate deep sleep, waking some time in the middle of the night with a desperate urge to go to the bathroom. Thank goodness it was en-suite, was her first thought. If she'd had to walk along the landing, Oliver might have pounced. She'd like to bet that he had one ear cocked listening for any sounds from her room.

She shivered as she threw off her clothes and pulled on a nightie, but once she had curled beneath the duvet she went straight back to sleep.

The next morning she was woken by Mrs Green with tea and biscuits. 'Eat these, my dear, and then lie down again for half an hour. You shouldn't feel sick then. It always worked with me.'

Anna struggled to sit up and pulled an embarrassed face. 'Oliver's told you?'

'Indeed he has. I'm very pleased for you both. I presume I should be pleased?'.

'We're back together,' said Anna quietly.

'But not in the same bed,' pointed out the housekeeper tartly. 'It's not a good sign. I have no idea what's gone on between you two but if you want my advice you'll patch things up, and quickly. Oliver's hopeful, I know. He was hell to live with when you went away. You two are made for each other. Don't throw your love away.'

When Anna finally made her way downstairs Oliver was waiting for her. She had hoped he'd be at work, she didn't want him disrupting his normal routine on her behalf, and she hoped it wasn't going to become a regular thing.

'What are you doing here?' she asked crossly as she walked into the breakfast room, yet at the same time her senses leapt in response to him, an awareness filling her that almost had her running into his arms.

'I've made an appointment for you at the doctor's,' Oliver informed her.

Anna felt a swift stab of resentment at the way he was taking over and was glad she hadn't given in to her urges. 'I'm quite capable of doing that for myself, thank you.'

'Yes, I know,' he answered, 'but I wasn't sure how quickly you'd do it and I thought that it was important you—'

'I don't need you to think for me,' she retorted.

And then decided that maybe she was being too hard on him. He still looked as though he hadn't slept in a month, although he was freshly showered and shaven, and he was wearing a crisp blue shirt with a pair of navy linen trousers. 'I'm sorry, of course you're concerned. When is the appointment?'

'Ten-thirty. We have plenty of time. Can you manage some breakfast now?'

'Maybe a slice of toast.'

Oliver frowned. 'That isn't much.'

'It's all I want,' she insisted. 'I remember my sister saying little had often suited her better than big meals.'

The doctor confirmed that she was indeed well and truly pregnant. He shook Oliver's hand and her own and wished them a healthy baby. 'It's a pity your father won't have the pleasure of seeing his grandchild.'

Oliver nodded curtly and outside the surgery Anna, having noticed his expression, said, 'That was a bit insensitive of him, talking about your father like that.'

'You don't know the half,' he muttered. 'My father wouldn't have wanted anything to do with his grandchild.'

'He wouldn't?' And then the ugly truth hit her. 'Because of me? Because he never liked me?' Goodness, had Edward's animosity gone that far? He would have spited his grandchild because he didn't approve of her?

'Of course not,' Oliver declared impatiently. 'Because he didn't like me. Get in the car and we'll talk at home, if you're really interested.'

Edward didn't like his son? This was news to Anna

and she pondered about it as Oliver drove. She'd never seen any signs. It didn't make sense.

In the house she turned to him. 'Tell me about your father. You've never hinted that there was anything wrong.'

Oliver drew in a deep breath and let it out slowly, ridding himself of some of his tension as they sat down.

'That's because we managed to rub along together,' he admitted with a heavy shrug. 'I respected him—it's something I was brought up to do. It's why I lived here instead of moving right away. He needed me, even though he wouldn't admit it. But that doesn't mean to say I'm not resentful of the way he used to treat me.'

'He didn't appreciate having to bring you up, is that what you're saying?'

'Something like that,' he admitted ruefully. 'I only went into the business to prove that I wasn't the idiot he always said I was. Even when he retired he couldn't accept that I was doing a good job. We had many arguments.'

And one of those arguments had resulted in his death, thought Anna sadly. She might not have liked Edward, and liked him even less now that she'd heard how he treated Oliver, but it didn't mean that she couldn't feel some sort of compassion for him.

She pulled a wry face. 'I suppose that explains the way he behaved towards me.'

'Not at all,' Oliver told her crisply. 'He married Rosemary in haste, without really getting to know her, and he thought he knew where we were heading. He would have accepted you in time.'

'No, he wouldn't,' replied Anna firmly. 'He actually offered me money not to marry you.'

'He did what?' Oliver jolted upright, golden eyes shocked. 'Why didn't you tell me?'

'Because I dealt with it,' she explained calmly. 'I tore up his cheque. I told him I loved you and it would have made no difference if you were a pauper.'

There was faint admiration in his eyes now. 'I bet he didn't like that.'

'I don't think he did.' Anna went quiet for a moment, wondering whether to tell him the rest.

'There's more, isn't there?'

She had forgotten how easily Oliver could read her mind, and her lips contorted themselves into a regretful smile. 'You know me too well.'

'So out with it. I might as well have the whole awful truth in one go.'

Anna swallowed hard. 'He threw me out. He told me it was his house and gave me a week to move.'

Oliver slumped. It was as though all the stuffing had been knocked out of him. 'And you went—without coming to see me? Without telling me what he'd done?'

Then, with a swift recovery, he bounced to his feet. 'The old bastard! Maybe it's as well you didn't tell me or I might have done something I later regretted. Anna—' he spoke more quietly now, struggling to control his powerful emotions '—why *didn't* you tell me?'

'I thought you wouldn't care,' she answered quietly. 'You'd never once been back to try and talk things over and I wasn't coming up there with your father in the house. I had too much pride for that.'

'So if my father hadn't died, we'd have never got back together. Is that what you're saying?'

'It's possible. I was hurting too much for a confrontation. You'd made up your mind and that was it.'

Oliver closed his eyes in self-recrimination. 'I don't know about calling my father a swine. I've been a pretty big one myself.'

'You can say that again.' But, despite all that had gone wrong between them, Anna still felt the strong pull of his sexuality. It was something that had never gone away, and she hated sitting here with distance between them. But sex wasn't the answer, she had to remember that. It was where they had gone wrong in the first place.

'Why didn't you ever tell me this house belonged to Edward?' she asked.

Oliver shrugged. 'I never gave it a thought. But I do think we should sell up soon. I think we should be settled into our new place before the baby is born.'

*Our new place! Our* new place. Was this a wise move? She had a lot of forgiving to do before commitments were made, and a new house meant commitment. It meant he was expecting her to spend the rest of her life with him.

'You don't look sure about it, Anna?' She hadn't realised he was watching her, nor that her face was so expressive. She shrugged. 'You said that if it didn't work out by the time the baby was born, then I'd be free to go. I don't see the point in us moving until we're sure that—'

Oliver's eyes flashed and he sprang to his feet. 'Maybe *you're* not sure, Anna, but I most definitely am. We are man and wife and that is the way I want us to stay.'

# CHAPTER TWELVE

ANNA'S first thought was that Oliver had tricked her. He had got her back here with the promise that she was free to leave if things didn't work out and now he was saying that he had no intention of letting her go.

'I love you, Anna,' he continued before she could respond. 'And I'd like to think that you still love me. The hurt hasn't yet gone away, which is understandable, but I have every intention of making amends for my atrocious behaviour. You will never again have cause to think ill of me. In fact, you'll thank me for coming after you.'

Her lips twisted wryly. 'That's a sweeping statement, Oliver.'

'I won't let you down, I promise,' he said urgently. 'Now I suggest that I find Mrs G and organise an early lunch. Are you feeling up to it?'

'Actually I am hungry,' she agreed, deciding there was no point in arguing. Only time would tell. 'I'll phone Chris while you're doing that. Let him know I'm back.'

He nodded. 'Good idea. Perhaps you ought to invite him over for dinner, one evening. It's about time I met this brother of yours.'

'You're not still of the opinion that Tony's lurking somewhere in the background?' The question was out before she could stop it.

Oliver groaned. 'Don't remind me how foolish I've been. I don't know why I thought he was involved. Well, yes, I do. You'd once said Tony was handsome and blond, and the guy my father saw you with matched that description. I never imagined that your brother would have blond hair.'

'Perhaps your mother leaving for such selfish reasons messed you up a lot,' she said. 'Made you suspicious of everyone.'

'It wasn't Rosemary leaving, it was my father's attitude,' he retorted bitterly.

Anna wanted to go to him then, to hold him, to say that everything would be all right. But she couldn't be sure. It was still far too early. How did she know Oliver wouldn't come down on her again when something else went wrong?

It wasn't easy, though, keeping her distance from him. In the weeks that followed Oliver became over protective, he was for ever asking how she was, if she needed anything, oughtn't she to rest more?

It was a constant bombardment and she was glad when he found it necessary to go to work.

He put both houses on the market and there began a steady stream of prospective purchasers. Anna kept out of the way whenever the agents came to show someone around.

Often she would go out looking for property that would be suitable for her and Oliver. 'I'll leave the choice entirely up to you,' he had said. 'If you're happy then I'll be happy.'

It was an onerous task, especially as she still wasn't sure whether their marriage would last. But at least it gave her something to do.

And when she happened upon a cottage deep in the Cambridgeshire countryside, a cottage that somehow reminded her of the cottage in Ireland where she and Oliver had been so deliriously happy, she knew that this was where she wanted to live.

It was crazy really, because why did she want reminders of a life that might have been? Or was she living in hope that one day things might work out between them? Was that really at the back of her mind?

The cottage wasn't for sale, so she didn't know why she had stopped to look. It was much bigger than the holiday cottage. It had probably started out in life as a two-up, two-down, but it had been extended over the years so that it was now as imposing as a country manor, and yet it still had that cottage appeal. Diamond-leaded windows and ivy clad walls, chimneys and gables and what looked like a massive garden for the children to play in.

Anna checked her thoughts. Children? Was she planning to have more children with Oliver? Had she subconsciously resigned herself to the fact that their marriage would get back on track?

She had no way of knowing. Half of her wanted it to happen; the other half was so deeply resentful of the way he had treated her that it was doubtful she would ever forgive him.

Even as she stood and looked at the cottage, smoke curled from one of the chimneys and Anna wanted to go and knock on the door and ask to be let in. She wanted to sit before a cosy log fire, warm her hands and her toes and dream that it was her very own house.

Over dinner that evening, she told Oliver about the cottage. 'It wasn't for sale but it's my dream house. I'd love to live somewhere like that.'

Her enthusiasm shone through and Oliver smiled appreciatively. 'If that's what you want, then that's what you shall have. Take me to see it and we'll start a search for a look-alike.'

And so on Sunday they drove out and when the elderly householder returned from taking his dog for a walk Oliver went to speak to him.

Anna got out of the car and stood and watched. She loved the cottage even more the second time. It was perfect. How would they ever find anything else like it?

Oliver came back. 'You're not going to believe this,' he said. 'But that guy's been thinking of selling for some time. It's too big for him, since his wife died, but he can't face the thought of a stream of strangers traipsing through. If we want it it's ours. He intends to go and live with his daughter in Essex.'

'Oh, Oliver!' Anna couldn't stop herself from flinging her arms around him. 'Does he mean it?'

'Absolutely. He said we can go inside and look now, if you like.'

'I don't care what it's like inside,' she said dismissively. 'I know it will be perfect. I can't believe we're so lucky.'

Oliver held her tightly against him, smiling indulgently into her glowing face. 'I've not seen you this happy since you came home.'

How it happened, she didn't know, but the next second Oliver's mouth possessed hers. It took her breath away, it sent a spiral of sensation through her entire body. And although she knew she ought to push him away, slap his face even, she somehow couldn't do it.

She let the kiss happen—in full view of the owner of the house. She let Oliver's mouth seduce hers into responding. She felt an elation that had been missing in her life for a long time.

It was a deeply satisfying kiss, a kiss that made her whole body throb and made her realise that she was punishing herself by shutting Oliver out. And when Oliver abruptly let her go she felt bereft.

She expected him to apologise, to declare that he had overstepped the mark, but he didn't. Instead he looked inordinately pleased with himself as he took her hand and led her up to the house.

Inside was as good as she'd expected, a well-proportioned living room and lounge, a dining room and a study, a kitchen to die for, and four bedrooms, two of them en-suite. It was perfect.

'What do you think?' asked the owner.

'It's fantastic,' said Anna. 'Exactly what we want. I can't believe we've been so lucky. Do you really want to sell?'

'I'd get out tomorrow if I could.'

'I'll see my solicitor first thing in the morning,' declared Oliver, and he held out his hand and they shook on the deal.

'I'm happy to let it go to two young people so obviously in love. It does my heart good to see you.' He was a white-haired, kindly-looking man. 'You remind me of my wife and myself when we were first married. We were kissing and cuddling the whole time. I hope you'll be as happy here as we were.'

Oliver's arm came about Anna's shoulders. 'I don't think there's any doubt about that.'

Anna felt a fraud but she lifted her face with the expected smile and Oliver kissed her. A brief kiss, this time, just a brushing of their lips for the old man's benefit, but it set her alight again and she wondered whether she was going to be able to keep up the game against Oliver for much longer.

'Do you like it as much as I do?' she asked when they returned to the car.

'No doubt about it,' he said, putting the key into the ignition and starting the engine. 'It will be a fresh start for both of us.'

But before he drove away he turned to her and said hopefully, 'Did your response to my kiss mean that you've finally forgiven me?'

Anna steeled her heart and shook her head. She couldn't give him false hopes. 'It was a moment of joy because of the cottage, nothing more.'

Brows lifted in disbelief. 'It didn't feel like nothing.'

'I'm not saying that my feelings for you have died, Oliver.' Far from it; they ran rampant all the time she and Oliver were together. 'But after the way you treated me, do you really expect me to jump back into your arms so quickly?' Her eyes flashed a vivid and scathing green. 'Actually, it might never happen. Having your own husband accuse you of stealing takes some getting over. Shall we go?'

He didn't say another word; he swung away and set the car in motion. A glance at his profile revealed a set jaw and beetling brows, and his grip on the steering wheel turned his knuckles white. Serves him right, she thought. He shouldn't throw stones without expecting to get hurt himself.

They didn't go straight home, as she'd expected; instead, Oliver took her to one of his favourite riverside restaurants for lunch. Anna no longer had bouts of morning sickness and was able to once more enjoy her food, so it was a treat to be taken out.

Fog hung over the water but there were people walking along the river bank wrapped warmly in scarves and hats and Anna watched them from their table near the window.

At first Oliver was quiet, deep in his own thoughts, making Anna wonder whether she had been unnecessarily hard on him. But why should she let him get away with what he had done? She was prepared to be friends for the sake of the baby, but no more, and it was best he knew that.

The fact that she was cutting off her nose to spite her face didn't enter into it. She could cope with having no one to kiss and cuddle her, no one to share her bed, no one to send her mindless with pleasure. Couldn't she?

She didn't like the answer her body gave, but sex wasn't the be-all and end-all of life. What if she hadn't got a husband or a boyfriend? She'd cope then, wouldn't she? Yes, but there was a difference when she shared a house with a man who had stolen her heart the first moment she set eyes on him.

'What are you thinking?'

Anna looked from the river to Oliver. She met the intenseness of his golden eyes and felt a dance of fire in her belly. 'Not much. This and that.'

'Would this and that be you and me, by any chance?' One dark eyebrow quirked knowingly.

Anna gave an inward groan. 'Maybe,' she acknowledged with a dismissive shrug of her slender shoulders.

'Are you regretting coming back to me?'

'No.' It was a tiny no, escaping swiftly before she had chance to think about it. But she didn't look at him, she played with her fork instead, moving a piece of potato around her plate, smashing it into tiny pieces. 'Not entirely.'

'Is there a chance that we'll get back on to the level that we so much enjoyed before I put my foolish foot in it?'

Still Anna didn't look at him, though she knew her answer would shape their future. It seemed as though he was beginning to think there was no hope. And did she really want that? Did she want to split up from him, go their separate ways, share their baby, toss it from one to the other over the years?

Her answer was most definitely no.

'I think we might, eventually,' she said in an almost whisper. But it wasn't now. She wasn't yet ready. How long it would take, she didn't know.

Oliver reached across the table and took her hand. 'If there is hope, then I can wait. Otherwise, I would prefer we ended it now.' Anna looked across and saw the pain in his eyes, the stark pain that was cutting right into him, and she almost gave in. But he needed to learn his lesson. She had to be hard for the sake of her future.

The fact that he'd apologised a thousand times— swore he would never accuse her of anything like that again—didn't altogether appease her. Words were easy; it was actions that counted.

So a few more weeks, perhaps, maybe even until the baby was born. But could she live with him for that long and still sleep in separate rooms? Already some of her resentment was wearing off; her traitorous body was reminding her of the fantastic times they'd had together, could have again.

'Anna?'

She realised that Oliver was still waiting for her answer. And, judging by the shadow darkening his face, by the rigid jut of his jaw, it looked as though he'd made up his mind that she wanted to leave.

'I'll stay with you, Oliver,' she said, her tone still quiet, 'but I need more time. I won't be rushed. If you do you'll drive me away.'

A great big smile chased the shadows from his face, his golden eyes lit up, and his hand tightened over hers. 'You won't regret this, Anna, I promise.'

She smiled faintly and gave her head an infinitesimal shake, as though not entirely sure of it herself. Tingles ran through her, congregating in a disturbing heat in the pit of her stomach. And all because he was holding her hand!

During the rest of the meal Oliver was his normal, cheerful, conversational self, and Anna found herself more relaxed than she had been in a long time. Perhaps the new house would be the answer.

Gone would be all the old memories, the old heartache. They would start again, and she'd have plenty to do arranging things, once they moved in. It didn't really need decorating but it would be nice to stamp her own personality on it.

'I was just thinking about the house,' she said. 'I still can't believe how lucky we are. It's so much of a coincidence that Mr Jones wanted to sell.'

'It must mean we were meant to have it,' Oliver claimed, eyes glowing with pleasure. 'Fate looked down on you that day, my sweetheart. It made you drive down that particular lane and made you stop and look at that particular cottage.'

Anna laughed. 'Oliver, I didn't realise you believed in such things.'

'I don't, as a rule, but what other explanation is there?' he asked, spreading his hands palms upward. 'What is to be will be—isn't that what they say?'

'Will Mrs Green come with us?'

'If you'd like her to. The idea of putting her out of a home and a job has been worrying me.'

'She's constantly talking to me about the baby,' said Anna. 'I think she's looking forward to helping me look after it.'

'It?' asked Oliver with mock indignance. 'You're calling my son an it?'

'Your son might be a daughter,' she pointed out.

He grinned. 'If she's as adorable as you, I'll be quite content. We'll have a boy next time.'

'And exactly how many children are you planning to have, Mr Langford?' But Anna didn't really mind this talk about babies. She liked to see Oliver happy. She hadn't realised how unhappy he had been, these last few weeks. She'd been so wrapped up in her own hurt that she'd hardly spared a thought for what he was going through.

'Oh, at least four,' he said airily, then raised a questioning brow. 'Of course, it all depends on whether I'm let back into your bed in time.'

Anna didn't answer that one, but she smiled as she sliced off a piece of tender lamb, dipping it into the delicious redcurrant sauce before popping it into her mouth.

Oliver watched her every move and when a speck of sauce dripped off the fork on to her chin he swiftly leant across the table and stroked it away with his finger. He then offered her his finger to suck away the offending drop.

At one time, Anna would have complied. They would have turned the whole event into a highly arousing sensual act. But although she was tempted, she wasn't quite up to that yet. He was rushing her. So she shook her head and Oliver, his lips twisting in wry disappointment, sucked his finger himself.

His eyes never left hers, though. He let her see that he was still getting pleasure out of tasting her drop of redcurrant sauce.

A tiny incident, and yet one that remained in Anna's mind for the rest of the day. In fact, this was the most enjoyable day she'd had in a long time.

After lunch they went for a drive and it was dark when they arrived home. She was laughing over something Oliver had said, wondering at the same time how she would be able to part from him when it was time for bed. They had shared so much today that she didn't want to let him go.

But her smile faded, and so did Oliver's, when they discovered a police car pulled up outside the house.

'What on earth—?' he exclaimed as he jumped out of the car and hurried forward.

Anna swiftly followed.

# CHAPTER THIRTEEN

OLIVER and Anna found Mrs Green entertaining two policemen in the kitchen. A teapot and a plate with one piece of shortbread and a few crumbs left on it was in front of them. They looked almost disappointed to be interrupted.

'What's going on?' asked Oliver, looking questioningly from one to the other.

'Mr Oliver Langford?' enquired the senior of the officers.

'That's right.'

'It's about Rosemary Langford—your mother, I believe?'

Oliver's eyes narrowed. 'I think you'd better come into my study.'

Anna wanted to follow but didn't feel she had the right, so she stayed behind with the housekeeper. 'What do they want? Did they say?'

Mrs Green pursed her lips. 'They wouldn't tell me. They've only been here about five minutes. Soon made short work of my shortbread, they did. One said he'd like the recipe for his wife.'

'Do you think anything's happened to Oliver's mother?' asked Anna worriedly.

'Can't say,' answered the housekeeper, and it was clear by her expression that she didn't really care. Rosemary Langford was Mrs Green's least favourite person.

It wasn't long before Anna heard Oliver showing the policemen out. She went straight to him. 'What's wrong? Is your mother ill?'

'No,' he answered fiercely. 'She's at the station. She's been arrested.'

'What?' Anna looked at him in wide-eyed shock. 'Why? What's she done?'

Oliver sucked in his cheeks as he appeared to be making a conscious decision how much to tell her.

'It's all right,' she said. 'It's your business. If you don't want to tell me, then—'

'I do want to tell you. I was wondering how to. But there is no way round it without putting myself in a bad light.'

Anna frowned. 'What are you talking about?'

'Rosemary stole the jewellery.'

'Oh!' For some reason, her legs grew weak and she groped for the chair behind her. No wonder Oliver had hesitated about telling her. He must feel even more of a first class fool now.

'Did she take it the night she stayed there, do you think?' she asked, a further puzzled frown drawing her fine brows together. It really was a disturbing matter. 'The night of your father's funeral?'

'No.' Oliver spoke very definitely. 'I saw them in the safe after that.'

'So, how did she do it?'

'That is something I intend to find out,' he answered grimly. 'I'm going to the police station right now. I don't know how long I'll be. Don't wait up.'

But Anna couldn't go to bed without knowing what was happening and when Oliver finally came home she was curled up on a chair in the sitting room with an open book on her lap, even though she wasn't reading.

Instead she'd been daydreaming, thinking about their future. In a month's time it would be Christmas—their first Christmas together. They wouldn't have moved by then, but next year they'd be well and truly settled in their new cottage and they'd have their baby to buy presents for. And hopefully all their troubles would be behind them.

Oliver looked tired and drained and surprised to see her still up.

'Can I get you a drink?' she asked. 'Mrs Green's gone to bed.'

But Oliver shook his head. 'You've had a long day. Shouldn't you be in bed also?'

'I wouldn't have been able to sleep without hearing about Rosemary. What's happened to her? Has she been charged?'

'No.' Oliver's lips were tight and grim as he sank down into the other armchair. Wearily, he stretched out his legs and, putting his head back, he looked at the ceiling.

'I couldn't let them do it to her.'

Because, after all, she was his mother. 'So they've let her go?'

'Yes.'

'And that's the end of it? You've got the jewellery back.'

'Not yet, but I will do.'

'You've spoken to Rosemary?'

'Briefly,' he admitted. 'I'm going to see her again in the morning.'

'How did she manage to get into the house?' asked

Anna, her mind working feverishly. 'Did she creep in while we were working upstairs?'

'I know none of the details yet. All I know is that I couldn't let them jail her. God knows why. She did me no favours, but—'

'It's because you're a decent and honorable man, Oliver Langford,' she told him quietly.

He sat up straight then and looked at her. 'You really mean that?'

'I guess I do,' she said, as if finding it surprising herself, 'but I'm still not rushing things.'

'I understand.' His expression was both sorrowful and hopeful. He stood up and came to her, and he pulled her to her feet and held her against him. There was nothing passionate about it. Like two friends greeting each other after a long absence.

Anna closed her eyes and let the warmth of him seep into her, the strength of him hold her upright, and the clean, familiar, masculine smell of him assault her nostrils.

It was a brief hug, disappointingly brief. And yet it was right that it should be so, because feelings were already being awoken inside her. Feelings she had clamped down, that were supposed to stay there until she gave them permission to flood back to life.

'Go to bed now, Anna,' he muttered, stroking a stray strand of hair from her brow with an incredibly gentle finger. 'Sleep well, my darling.'

Anna wanted to ask if he was going to bed too but, afraid that he might interpret it as an invitation, she headed for the door, turning as she went through it to give him a sad smile. 'I'm sorry about your mother.'

The following day when Oliver went to see

Rosemary, Anna took the opportunity to go up to the Hall to have a last look around.

All of Edward's personal belongings had now been sorted and what needed to be got rid of had gone. Everything was ready for the sale. There was even a middle-aged couple very interested in it. Strangely, Anna felt sad that it would soon pass out of the Langford family.

And yet she could understand Oliver wanting to have nothing further to do with it. Her own childhood memories were so happy that she found it hard to imagine any father treating his son the way Edward had treated Oliver.

Every time he came up here, he must remember the misery of his childhood. She could feel his pain, suffer for him, and yet hadn't he forced her to suffer too? Was there something of his father in him that reared its ugly head every now and then? Ought she still to be careful?

She heard footsteps and couldn't help speculating why she wasn't surprised when Melanie appeared.

'I wondered who was in here,' said the other girl abruptly. 'I hoped it was Oliver.'

'I'm sorry to disappoint you.' Anna eyed the blonde suspiciously.

'Is he with you?'

'No.'

'Is he at work?'

Anna had no intention of telling Melanie where Oliver was. It was up to him whether he told her what Rosemary had done. 'Actually, he has business to attend to. Is there anything in particular you wanted him for? Shall I tell him you called?'

'I want to know why he is selling this house,' declared Melanie aggressively. 'Why he didn't tell me what he was planning. I did wonder why he was packing all Uncle Edward's stuff up but I thought it was because he was going to move in himself.' A scowl creased her brow. 'I bet it's all your doing. I bet—'

'Melanie,' Anna interrupted firmly, 'it has nothing to do with me. It was Oliver's decision. If you have a problem with it then I suggest you ask him.'

'Oh, I intend to,' she snapped. 'Your marriage still isn't going to work out, you know. He told me he's getting a little fed up of the way you're messing him about.'

'Is that so?' Anna wondered what Melanie would have to say if she knew that Anna was pregnant. Thank goodness it was too soon for her to show. 'Then answer me this, Melanie,' she said coolly. 'If that's the way he feels, why did he come after me?'

Melanie shrugged. 'Oliver's like that. Actually, no man likes to think he's been dumped; they like to do the dumping.'

'I see,' said Anna stiffly. 'Thank you for telling me. I'll bear it in mind, the next time I feel like walking out. And I'll tell him you called. Goodbye, Melanie.'

With a toss of her long blonde hair, Melanie turned and walked out. Anna shivered. Wasn't that girl ever going to get the message?

It was way past lunchtime when Oliver returned. Anna had presumed he'd gone straight to the office after visiting Rosemary and she'd accepted that she wouldn't see him again until evening. She was unprepared for the rush of warmth that enveloped her.

Whether it was because of Melanie's comments,

whether it was because of the kiss yesterday, or whether it was because she really was beginning to forgive him, she wasn't sure. But whatever, her reaction to him was almost like that in the early days of their marriage.

And it must have shown on her face because Oliver looked at her hesitantly and then took her into his arms. 'You almost look pleased to see me,' he said, still not attempting to kiss her, but holding her with the tenderness that only a man in love could.

'I am. I want to know what's gone on.'

'Is that all?' He held her at arm's length, but there was no censure in his voice. A smile perhaps, indulgence. 'First of all, tell me how you are. As a matter of fact, Mrs Langford, now that your morning sickness has passed, you're beginning to look more radiant with each passing day.'

'I feel good,' she admitted. 'I went up to the Hall this morning. You didn't mind?' she asked, as a faint after thought.

'Not at all. Did we have more viewers? I thought Mr—'

'No, I just wanted to look at it, to picture you there as a child. I—'

He put his finger gently over her lips. 'Let's not talk about that.'

'I had a visitor while I was there.'

He frowned then. 'Who?'

'Melanie.'

And his arms dropped to his sides. 'What did she want?' He moved away from her, went to stand by the fireplace where a log fire was burning. Oliver always liked a real fire in the room they used most, despite the central heating.

'She wanted you.'

'What for?'

'I have no idea,' Anna admitted. 'I said I'd tell you she'd been.'

'Right, well, I'll deal with it.' He spoke matter-of-factly, as though it were some business matter he was dealing with, but Anna couldn't help wondering exactly how much Melanie meant to him.

'Tell me about Rosemary.' Anna sat down and tucked her legs beneath her in a corner of the settee.

Oliver dropped into an armchair but he couldn't relax. He sat forward, legs parted, hands linked between them, staring at the pattern on the carpet.

He had felt bad enough about accusing Anna but now that he had absolute, positive proof that she hadn't taken the heirlooms he felt a hundred times worse. How was he ever going to face her again? How was he ever going to make amends?

'She stole a key,' he said shortly. 'My father was a creature of habit; he kept them in the same place as thirty years ago. And then she enlisted Melanie's help to get us both out of the house.'

'Oh! That was the day I went to see Chris the day—' She stopped abruptly.

'The day I thought you'd had the opportunity to take them. Yes, I know.' He shook his head, his shoulders bowed. 'How could I have got things so dreadfully wrong, Anna?'

'I suppose it was a natural conclusion.'

And how could she be so understanding after the

way he'd treated her? Admittedly, she hadn't yet totally forgiven him, but she was definitely weakening. When she responded to his kiss yesterday, he had felt as though he'd won the lottery. Not the big win, but a very satisfying win nevertheless.

'No, it wasn't a natural conclusion,' he admitted unhappily. 'It was like firing a gun without looking at the target. It was insanity.'

'We're supposed to be discussing Rosemary, not me,' she said firmly. 'What was her reaction when you said you weren't going to press charges? I hope she was properly grateful.'

'I don't think she even thought it would get as far as her being charged,' he confessed unhappily. 'She was busy trying to convince the officers that the jewellery was rightfully hers because she was still legally next of kin to Edward.'

'Did it work?'

'Not when I said he'd left her precisely nothing in his will and that it had been thirty years since they'd lived together. But, much as I despise Rosemary, I couldn't let her go to prison. So long as I get the stuff back, then I'm prepared to take it no further.'

'She's very lucky.'

Oliver shrugged. 'Surprisingly, I feel sorry for her. She made a big mistake when she walked out on my father and me and I think she realises that now. She's left with no family and only a handful of friends—if she can even call them that. It's not exactly an inviting picture for her old age.'

'So she wanted to make sure she had a little nest egg, is that it?'

'I guess so.'

'Was she planning to sell the stuff?'

'Yes.'

'I think I feel sorry for her as well.'

Anna was magnificent, decided Oliver. Only the very purest person could forgive a woman who had unwittingly caused her a great deal of hurt. He desperately wanted to go to her, to hold her, to never let her out of his arms again—ever.

But he had to be careful, he still needed to take things one step at a time. Too much pushing now and he would be back to square one. In fact, it could push her away altogether.

'I told her about the new house,' he admitted. 'I told her she was welcome to visit any time she wanted.'

Anna lifted her brows in surprise. 'That was very generous of you.'

'She is my mother,' he admitted with a wry twist of his lips.

'Most men would turn their back on her, especially after this latest episode.'

'Maybe I would have done, once. You're the one who's made me realise that it is possible to forgive, no matter how bad the crime.'

Anna didn't answer and he didn't blame her. Instead she jumped to her feet. 'I'll go and ask Mrs Green to make us a pot of tea. Have you had lunch? There's some excellent chicken soup that—'

'I'm not hungry,' he interrupted. 'Just the tea—or coffee, I think. Whatever you're having.'

Anna smiled. 'Camomile tea, then?'

He groaned and clapped a hand comically to his

brow, having forgotten that she'd gone off ordinary tea. 'Not that stuff, please. I'll have coffee.'

When she'd gone, he leant back in his chair and closed his eyes. His talk with Rosemary had drained him, but he was glad that they'd reached some sort of compromise. He didn't particularly want to be close to her—he didn't want her taking advantage of him—but on the other hand no mother deserved the cold shoulder from her son, no matter what she had done.

In truth, he couldn't clearly remember her from his childhood. He recalled a vague figure who always smelt nice and wore sparkling earrings, but that was all. It was his father's attitude that had kept alive his resentment—and, now Edward had gone, what was the point in remaining hostile?

But his thoughts didn't remain with his mother for very long. Anna was his main concern, Anna and the baby. He couldn't begin to describe how he felt about the fact that he was going to become a father.

It was a scary thought as well as an exciting one. He knew nothing about bringing up babies, or even about children in general. He'd always steered well clear of them. It was probably his own experiences that had done this to him, but the time had come for him to learn.

He'd already said he would go with Anna to her antenatal classes but he really wanted to learn more. Or did being a father come naturally? Perhaps a book on child care would be beneficial?

'What are you thinking?'

He hadn't heard Anna re-enter the room. He

opened one eye. 'About being a father.' And closed it again quickly.

'You think it's not manly to think about it?'

'It frightens me half to death.'

'Me too,' she admitted.

Immediately he opened both eyes and looked at her. 'You've nothing to be afraid of. I'll be there for you every step of the way.'

And to his enormous pleasure she came and sat on his lap. The first time she had voluntarily come to him. It almost took his breath away and he had to force himself not to read too much into it, not to smother her with love and kisses, not to scare her away again.

'I know you'll look after me, Oliver,' she said in a breathy little whisper.

'For ever,' he assured her.

And they sat like that in quiet, reassuring silence. He was afraid to do more than hold her gently, and also afraid she would feel his response to her nearness. He felt on fire, everything throbbing, everything wanting. Hunger so intense that it hurt. He didn't know for how long he could carry on being a gentleman, but he didn't want to be the first to break away.

It was a bittersweet relief when Mrs Green came in with their drinks. They both sprang guiltily apart. Though why, he didn't know except that's how he felt. Guilty. It was probably because his housekeeper knew full well what their sleeping arrangements were. What would she make of this?

The woman said nothing but her smile was broad as she looked at him. 'Here we are. Your favourite fruit cake as well.' And there was a lift to her step as she turned and went out.

'She thinks we're back together,' said Anna.

'It's a nice thought.'

'But a premature one. Cake, Oliver?'

The interlude was over. The first tiny step taken. She was not going to let him overstep the mark. But he nevertheless felt more hopeful than he had in a long time.

# CHAPTER FOURTEEN

OLIVER held out his hand. 'I'm pleased to meet you at last.'

The other man shook it firmly. 'Me too. I'd begun to think it would never happen.'

They eyed each other squarely—two tall men, both broad-shouldered and good-looking, one dark haired, one blond. Anna kept her eye on Oliver, but there was no hint of suspicion. Oliver truly was pleased to meet her brother and she could tell by the warmth of his smile that he now accepted Chris without reservation.

'I'm glad also that you've met at last,' she said, her voice fired with enthusiasm. 'You spend so much time away from home these days, Chris, that you're difficult to track down.'

He shook his head in dismissal. 'You can always get in touch with me, sis, you should know that. It's a big contract I've landed in France; I can't afford to neglect them.'

'Of course not,' commented Oliver. 'Business is business. What would you like to drink? Scotch? Gin? Vodka?'

'Scotch, please, with just a dash of water.'

'And a mineral water for you, Anna?' he asked, his eyes softening as he looked at her.

'Please.'

'Have you told your brother our good news?'

She smiled and nodded happily, and Chris said, 'I've already given Anna my congratulations. I'm happy for you both.'

'We're happy, too,' agreed Oliver as he busied himself at the drinks cupboard. 'It's the best thing that could have happened to us.' He threw a meaningful look at Anna as he spoke and she felt a quick surge of pure pleasure. She knew that he was trying to tell her that if she hadn't gotten pregnant they might easily have gone their separate ways.

'My sales team tell me that your ad campaign and your attention to detail has been second to none, Chris,' said Oliver handing him his drink. 'Business is booming as a result of it. Good man.'

'Without my little sister's generosity, I'd never have made it,' Chris answered firmly. 'I have something for you, Anna.' He withdrew an envelope from his inside pocket and handed it to her. 'A cheque for the full amount of the loan. I was going to wait until the end of the evening, but since we're talking business I think you should have it now.'

'Thank you,' she said quietly. 'There was no rush.' And she would rather he hadn't done it in front of Oliver, although she guessed that it was deliberate. She had the feeling that Chris was trying to goad Oliver into apologising again.

And it worked.

'You make me feel the world's biggest heel, Chris,' he said with a short laugh. 'It's a pity I didn't meet you when we were first married. I'd have known then that I had nothing to worry about. I somehow got you confused with Anna's ex-fiancé.'

'Tony?' Chris raised his eyebrows. 'I saw him the

other day, did I tell you, Anna? He's married a rich, young widow. Her husband owned a growing chain of supermarkets. He had no relatives, so she became the very wealthy new owner. Tony's having the time of his life.'

Anna felt Oliver watching for her response, but all she did was laugh. 'So he's got his money without working for it. Amazing. He's someone else who attaches importance to money. It should never enter into relationships. I know when I met...' She tailed off, looking at Oliver from beneath her lashes. 'Forget I said that. It's not important.'

Chris frowned as he looked from one to the other. 'Is there something I'm missing, here? I thought all was hunky dory between you two again.'

'Not quite,' admitted Oliver. 'Your sister's playing hard to get, these days.'

'With a baby on the way?' Chris lifted a questioning brow at Anna.

'It makes life less predictable,' she said with a light laugh. 'Shall we go through to the dining room? I'm sure Mrs Green has everything ready.'

Chris had been going to bring his new girlfriend along tonight but at the last minute she'd been unable to come, so Anna was landed with the two men. A few weeks ago it would have been unthinkable, unbearable, but gradually she and Oliver had drawn closer until she was now almost ready to forgive him.

Almost but not quite.

Next week it was Christmas. Maybe the best Christmas present ever would be to give herself to him. Finally and irrevocably.

She smiled at the thought, and felt a swift surge of

longing deep in her stomach. Could she really wait? The way she was feeling at the moment she wanted to jump on him the second her brother left. She wanted to share his bed, to experience once more a magical night of lovemaking.

'You're looking mighty pleased with yourself, all of a sudden,' Oliver said, glancing at her across the table. 'Are you going to share whatever's brought that smile to your face?'

He never missed a trick. He was always watching her, even when she wasn't aware of it. And quite often he anticipated her needs. He loved her so much, and he wasn't afraid to show it, that she sometimes felt guilty for still keeping him at arm's length. Thank goodness he didn't know *exactly* what she was thinking.

'I'm just happy my brother's here,' she said lightly, hugging the warm glow that enveloped her. 'I'm glad you two have met at last. It's a pity Laura couldn't come. We'll have to meet her some other time, Chris.'

And she remained happy and excited for the whole of the meal. Oliver and Chris got on well, making Anna realise that if business crises hadn't kept the two men apart, her marriage problems would have been solved a whole lot earlier.

On the other hand, she and Oliver had now earned each other's trust; their ups and downs had been a learning curve, one more step on life's difficult staircase.

When Chris finally left, she and Oliver made themselves comfortable in the sitting room. It was Anna's favourite room with its deep armchairs and cosy fire.

Even in the summer she liked it because of the glorious views over the open countryside.

'I'm glad you and Chris got on well,' she said, leaning her head back, and folding her hands over her slightly swollen tummy.

Oliver inclined his head. 'He's a good man. Brilliant brain. It would have been a shame if his business had gone under.'

'That's what I thought,' she said, covertly studying him from beneath almost closed eyes. He was so gorgeous, so sexy, so desirable—nothing had changed.

All animosity had left her. She wanted him so desperately, it hurt. Why wait till Christmas? Why wait another whole seven days? Why carry on torturing herself?

On the other hand, the wait would be worth it. She'd walk into his room on Christmas morning and climb into his bed. It would be a present he'd remember for the rest of his life.

'I'm proud of you for keeping your promise to your brother.'

She looked at him then, green eyes openly questioning. 'You are?'

'Absolutely. It couldn't have been easy.'

'You can say that again.'

'Especially as it put our marriage in jeopardy,' he said gruffly.

'I would have actually told you if you hadn't offended me by checking my bank account and jumping to all the wrong conclusions.' She lifted her fine brows in censure. 'That was despicable, Oliver.'

'I know,' he admitted guiltily. 'But my father was convinced you'd only married me for my money. I wanted to prove him wrong—it's why I checked your account. I saw red when it had all gone.' He raked his fingers through his hair and dropped his forehead into his palm, hiding his face from her in self-disgust. 'I couldn't think why you had any need to take it. I couldn't think straight, if the truth's known.'

'So it was Edward again who put a spoke in our marriage,' she confirmed sharply. 'I rather thought it might have been. He must have permanently spied on me, looking for something to blacken me in your eyes. He succeeded magnificently.'

'I'm so sorry,' said Oliver, and she could see the pain etched in his face.

'Me, too,' she admitted.

'Am I forgiven yet?'

Anna smiled, secretly thinking about Christmas. 'I'm getting there.'

'Are you close enough to give me a goodnight kiss?' he asked hoarsely.

Yes please, clamoured her heart. She smiled, faintly. 'I think I could manage that.'

'Come here, then.'

Slowly, as if drawn by an invisible cord, Anna pushed herself up and closed the space between them. Arms reached out for her and she was pulled gently down on to his lap. Then those same arms held her possessively and she lifted her head to look into smouldering gold eyes.

It was almost her undoing. She found herself wanting more than a kiss—she wanted Oliver, all of him, here, now. And he wanted her! There was no ignoring his arousal. She was sitting on it!

But incredibly his kiss was gentle. It was tentative,

it was exploratory, it was humble, it was hopeful. It was so many things. His hands didn't rove, his tongue didn't beg. But even without passion he set her on fire.

Nevertheless, Anna decided to call a halt. Those extra few days' breathing space would heighten the pleasure and excitement. And it would do him good to worry a little while longer.

'I'm off to bed now, Oliver,' she said lightly.

He didn't argue, he didn't detain her, but he looked woefully unhappy and Anna knew that, for all his outward patience, all his repeated apologies, he was suffering badly—and that if she pushed him too hard for too long he might think it wasn't worth it and call the whole thing off.

Maybe waiting for Christmas wasn't such a good idea after all. Maybe now would...

But already he was helping her to her feet. 'You're usually in bed by this time. What am I thinking? Good night, sweetheart. Pleasant dreams.'

'Goodnight, Oliver.' She reached up and kissed him again—the first really spontaneous kiss in a long time. And when she lay in bed a short time later Anna found herself riddled with doubts.

Oliver had paid the penalty. The time had come for her to forgive and forget, to welcome him with open arms into her bed again. It felt so empty and cold without him, despite the electric blanket.

She wouldn't need a blanket with Oliver. He would warm her, body and soul—he would set her on fire. Another whole week of sleeping alone in this bed was going to be sheer purgatory.

The next couple of days she was so busy with last-minute Christmas shopping, decorating the tree she had insisted Oliver buy, bringing in armfuls of holly, doing all the hundred and one things that Christmas entailed, that she fell exhausted into bed each night. And Oliver laid no claims on her either, which was a help although it also surprised her.

She had thought that he would want to press home his advantage, repeat the kisses, turn it into something more. But no, he contented himself with a brief kiss each night, a kiss that meant absolutely nothing, a kiss that made her extremely disappointed—and also frustrated if the truth were known.

Two days before Christmas Oliver had a business dinner to attend. 'I'll probably be late back,' he said, 'so don't wait up.'

That was another night taken care of.

And on Christmas Eve night Melanie paid them a visit.

She brought a present for Oliver but nothing for Anna. Not that Anna minded, she hadn't bought Melanie anything either. And she was surprised when Oliver told the other girl that he had something for her.

'It's upstairs. I'll go and get it,' he said.

Melanie warmed her hands in front of the fire after he'd gone. 'We had a good time last night at the dinner. Did Oliver tell you?'

The words were calculatingly casual but Anna felt as though she'd been kicked in the stomach, as though all the breath had been knocked out of her. And her first thought was, thank goodness I didn't go to bed with Oliver.

Her second thought was that she couldn't blame

him for turning to Melanie when she wouldn't give him what he wanted. And it answered her question as to why he was so patient.

And her third thought was that she mustn't let Melanie see how surprised and hurt she was.

'Of course Oliver told me,' she replied in what she hoped was her normal voice. It didn't quite sound like it, but maybe Melanie wouldn't notice.

'We went back to my place afterwards. Oliver—'

'Melanie!'

The colour drained from Melanie's face as Oliver's appalled voice came from the doorway. 'What the hell are you talking about?'

Melanie turned slowly to face him but her eyes didn't quite meet his.

'Do you always talk like this to my wife when my back's turned?'

The blonde girl pouted and shrugged.

'Anna?'

But Anna didn't want to get involved and so she remained silent also.

'Believe me, Anna,' Oliver said, 'There is nothing going on between Melanie and myself. Not a thing, not for a long time.' He crossed the room to Anna's side and draped his arm about her shoulders.

'This is my wife, Melanie, and I love her very much. I'd like you to remember that. Whatever we once had going between us has been over a long time, and if you're going to come here to cause trouble then I'd prefer you didn't visit again.'

A slow burn flamed Melanie's face and without saying another word she turned and walked out.

'You didn't give her her present,' Anna reminded him quietly.

'She doesn't deserve it,' he said harshly. 'Does she speak to you like that often?'

'Only every time we meet.'

He groaned and his arm about her tightened. 'I had no idea. I hope you don't believe her because there's not a word of truth in it.'

'I used to,' she admitted, enjoying the feel of his hard body against her.

'It really was a business dinner. I don't know how Melanie found out about it.'

'I believe you,' she said.

'Oh, Anna, my Anna.' He held her against him for a long throbbing moment. 'What you've had to put up with. I'm so sorry. There's been nothing between me and Melanie since that day I found her bragging. I've felt it a duty to keep an eye on her for my father's sake, but that's all. I don't think I ever really loved her—not the way I love you.'

It was time.

The message rang loud and clear in Anna's head.

Time to tell Oliver.

No point in waiting until tomorrow.

The time was now.

## CHAPTER FIFTEEN

OLIVER had felt appalled when he stood listening to Melanie's lies. All he could think of was what it was doing to do to Anna, how it was in danger of wrecking their still fragile relationship.

He'd worked so hard over the last weeks to ensure nothing went wrong. It was half killing him to hold back, to remain patient and attentive, when what he really wanted to do was ravish her lovely body, made even lovelier by the fact that she was carrying his baby.

This don't-touch-me rule was driving him insane. And the number of times he'd almost lost control and demanded to know how much longer she was going to keep it up were nobody's business. Only the fact that he knew he would ruin everything if he did stopped him.

But how long was a man expected to wait?

As he continued to hold Anna, his whole body burnt with a fierce flame and he didn't want to let her go. Another night in bed alone, another night of tormented dreams, and then waking on Christmas morning with no one in bed beside him. How could he bear it?

'Oliver,' Anna whispered urgently. 'I'd like to give you your Christmas present now. Will you wait here while I fetch it?'

He smiled down at her. 'Of course, but I thought we'd put them under the tree and—'

'This is only a part of it.'

'If it's what you want.'

She looked so eager all of a sudden, her eyes alight, her lips parted in anticipation. And so damned sexy, more like the girl he'd first met. Her vitality had been missing, she'd become serious and withdrawn, and it was a pleasure to see her like this again.

He wondered what the present was that she couldn't wait to give him. She looked so excited that he knew he daren't let her down, even if he didn't like it although he was sure he would since it was Anna's choice.

He stood with his back to the fire, his hands behind him feeling its warmth. He heard her light footsteps on the stairs and saw the door coming open.

After that he was robbed of speech, robbed of breath, robbed of everything.

All Anna wore was a short, sheer red nightdress decorated with gold tinsel. There was a big green and red bow in her hair and high-heeled green sandals on her feet also decked out with tinsel.

She was all seductress as she sashayed towards him, her shining emerald eyes locked into his. His heart hammered frenziedly against his breast bone, pulses pounded, but apart from that he couldn't move a muscle, not even blink.

He was completely mesmerised by this exquisite creature who came up to him and slid her arms around him and said the words he thought he would never hear again.

'Oliver, I love you. I forgive you; I'm now ready to be yours.'

He swallowed hard. '*You* are my present?'

'If you want me.'

'If I want you?' There was no doubt about that. He'd nearly died with wanting her. 'Oh, Anna,' he groaned. 'Anna. This is the best Christmas present ever.' And his head swooped and he found her mouth and this time there was no holding back, no reservations—on his part or Anna's.

Anna had almost forgotten what it was like to be loved by Oliver, forgotten the excitement that trembled through her veins, the heat that invaded her limbs, the hunger that took over.

His tongue probed with an urgency that thrilled her, it explored intimately and fiercely what had long been denied him. Oliver the lover came back to life, ruthlessly demanding, passionately taking, and her own desires leapt in abandoned response.

She could actually feel his hands trembling as they sought the contours of her body beneath the thin red layers of fabric, slightly hesitant, as though he was still a fraction uncertain.

He didn't need to be. She was his now for all time, and she wanted to reassure him. 'I really do love you, Oliver, very, very much.'

His golden eyes were dark with desire as he raised his head, his mouth was soft and moist from her own mouth. 'You've truly forgiven me?' he asked thickly.

'Totally,' she whispered. 'If I carried on the feud any longer, I'd be torturing myself.'

'Oh, Anna,' he groaned, 'you don't know how I've

longed to hear you say that. This is the best day of my entire life.'

'Let's go to bed,' she suggested quietly and huskily.

His eyes gleamed with fresh desire. 'Can I unwrap my Christmas present in bed?'

'Yes.'

'Can I play with my present all night long?'

'Yes.'

'Then let's go,' he said with a triumphant grin. 'Let's not waste a minute.' He swung her up into his arms and Anna felt the unsteady beat of his heart as he carried her upstairs to his bedroom. She felt the intense heat of his body, the urgency that fuelled him.

And it was fuelling her! This was better than when they'd first met. It had been exciting then, yes, but this was a different excitement. She knew her man, now—she knew what to expect, she knew his hard-boned body as well as her own. She knew how much he could pleasure her and she could pleasure him.

But in this Anna was mistaken. Everything was so much better than she remembered, and it all began when Oliver untied the bow in her hair.

'Rule number one,' he informed her with a slow, teasing smile, 'never tear your wrappings. Always undo with care.' The ribbon came off and was neatly folded for further use. Next he cradled her face between his palms and kissed every inch of it, slowly and thoroughly, eyelids, nose, the incredibly erogonous zone behind her ears which made her wriggle and moan, and finally he claimed her mouth.

A long slow kiss, as though he had all the time in the world. He nibbled her lips, he dropped kisses inside her lower lip; his tongue explored, it danced attendance on her own, it created havoc with her senses.

When he finally lifted his head there was a glittering satisfaction in his golden eyes. 'Rule number two,' he said. 'Make the pleasure last. Explore the gift's shape before you unwrap it completely.'

They were standing in front of the mirrored wardrobe and he stepped behind her so that she could watch every move he made—and her reaction to him.

His hands began at her throat, stroking a slow and tantalising path towards her breasts. Her head fell back against his shoulder, her breathing grew quicker and shallower, and her eyes watched with greedy fascination.

Her breasts had grown fuller during her pregnancy and were sometimes too sensitive to touch, but at this moment they ached with need, and when his large capable hands closed over them she gave a tiny moan of pleasure.

Watching through the mirror, Anna saw the way her body wriggled against him, the luminous green of her eyes, the way her face screwed up as though she were in pain. Except that the pain was pleasure—a deep, unadulterated, long-awaited pleasure.

All this she had been missing; all this he had almost thrown away. It was unthinkable.

His hands moved lower, over her rounded hips, over her slightly swollen stomach. It was his turn to give a groan of pleasure at that point, and finally he reached the hem of her nightdress.

Anna waited with bated breath for rule number three.

She tried to guess what it would be. Perhaps something like—Finally, pull off the wrapper with equal care. Fold it up carefully before proceeding.

It never came.

Oliver suddenly couldn't wait. Her nightdress was yanked over her head and their eyes met in the mirror for one brief heart-stopping second before he effortlessly picked her up and carried her across to the bed.

It was then a race to get out of his own clothes. It took him about five seconds before he landed on the bed beside her.

'Do you like your gift?' she asked with a mischievous smile.

'Do I like it?' he groaned. 'What a question.'

'I was going to wait until morning, but suddenly I couldn't.'

'I'm glad,' he said roughly. 'I wasn't looking forward to waking up on Christmas morning with my wife in another room. I think I might have come in and ravished you anyway.'

'I'm glad we're friends again, Oliver,' she said, snuggling against him.

'Tonight you're not my friend, you're my lover— my very charming, my very enchanting, my very beautiful, my very pregnant lover.'

'Take me, Oliver,' she urged. 'Make me yours again.'

'It won't hurt the baby?'

'No. He needs to know that he's loved, too.'

Oliver needed no further encouragement. They lay stomach to stomach, hip to hip, and when he entered her it was with such loving care that it was Anna who went a little wild, Anna who rolled him on to his back, straddling him, riding him, feeling herself go mindless with pleasure when her climax came.

The next time it was his turn to kneel over her, his turn to take the lead, to bring her to a peak of desire before he finally gave her the release she begged.

Most of the night they continued to play their love games. It was almost as though they were making up for lost time. But eventually exhaustion set in; their eyes closed, their bodies grew limp and sleep claimed them.

And when they awoke it was snowing outside.

As it never—or very rarely—snowed on Christmas morning, Anna saw this as a good omen. 'Look,' she said, rubbing a circle in the condensation on the window and peering outside. 'Look, Oliver. Isn't it wonderful?'

'I think you're wonderful. I would never have forgiven me for what I did.'

'Isn't there some corny old saying about love conquering all? I guess I never truly stopped loving you.'

'Nor I you,' he said. 'Come here, Anna, and let me prove it to you.'

She didn't need any persuasion, and if it hadn't been for Mrs Green cooking their Christmas dinner Anna and Oliver Langford would probably have stopped in bed for the rest of the day.

# EPILOGUE

*Two years later…*

'I THINK we ought to go on honeymoon.' Oliver, lying in bed beside Anna, ran his hand over her swollen abdomen. 'Before Junior Two puts in his appearance.'

Anna smiled slowly. 'Mmm, I think I'd like that. Where shall we go?'

'Somewhere exotic and hot where all you have to do is lie around all day and be deliciously lazy.'

'I can't imagine myself ever being lazy,' she murmured.

They had moved house before Peter was born and although Mrs Green did all she could Anna really liked doing most things herself.

She loved looking after her darling baby and her gorgeous husband. She went cold every time she thought about how near she had come to losing him. And of course she loved her new house.

When Peter was ten months old they'd added an annexe to the cottage—Rosemary was coming to live with them!

Oliver's mother had changed. Her fright with the police and Oliver's unexpected generosity had made her do a lot of hard thinking. And today she was a gracious lady who had finally accepted that there was more to life than money.

'Do you know where I'd like to go?' Anna said,

stroking Oliver's cheek, feeling the early morning
rasp of a much needed shave.

'The world's your oyster, my darling. Just name
it.'

'To Dawn's cottage. We were so happy there,
Oliver. It would be a perfect place for a honeymoon.
And now your mother's here, I'm sure she'll help Mrs
Green look after Peter.'

'I think you're right,' he said. 'She's really taken
to the little guy. She says he reminds her of me at his
age. I don't think she wants to miss out on his childhood the way she did mine.'

'So it's settled?' she asked, eyes shining.

'If that's what you really want?'

'I do, more than anything in the world. And Oliver,
thank you for loving me.'

'Oh, no,' he said quickly, 'it's me who has to thank
you for giving me a second chance. And it has
worked out, hasn't it?'

Anna nodded. 'Better than I ever expected. I'm the
happiest woman in the world.'

'And I,' he said with the widest grin imaginable,
'am the happiest man.'

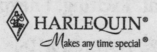

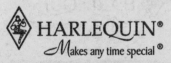

# HARLEQUIN *Presents*

**The world's bestselling romance series...
The series that brings you your favorite authors,
month after month:**

Helen Bianchin...Emma Darcy
Lynne Graham...Penny Jordan
Miranda Lee...Sandra Marton
Anne Mather...Carole Mortimer
Susan Napier...Michelle Reid

## and many more uniquely talented authors!

Wealthy, powerful, gorgeous men...
Women who have feelings just like your own...
The stories you love, set in exotic, glamorous locations...

HARLEQUIN *Presents*

## Seduction and passion guaranteed!

# HARLEQUIN®
# INTRIGUE

## WE'LL LEAVE YOU BREATHLESS!

If you've been looking for thrilling tales of
contemporary passion and sensuous love stories
with taut, edge-of-the-seat suspense—then
you'll love Harlequin Intrigue!

Every month, you'll meet four new heroes
who are guaranteed to make your spine tingle
and your pulse pound. With them you'll enter
into the exciting world of Harlequin Intrigue—
where your life is on the line
and so is your heart!

## THAT'S INTRIGUE—
## ROMANTIC SUSPENSE
## AT ITS BEST!

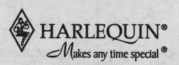

HARLEQUIN®

*Makes any time special* ®

**Harlequin® Historical**

*From rugged lawmen and valiant knights to defiant heiresses and spirited frontierswomen, Harlequin Historicals will capture your imagination with their dramatic scope, passion and adventure.*

*Harlequin Historicals... they're too good to miss!*

HHDIR1